THE PAINTER OF SIGNS

R. K. Narayan was born in Madras, ... in 1906, and educated there and at Maharaja's C... e. His first novel, *Swami and Friends* (1935), and ... *The Bachelor of Arts* (1937), are both set in the en... ial territory of Malgudi. Other 'Malgudi' novels are ... *Room* (1938), *The English Teacher* (1945), *Mr Sampath* (194... *ne Financial Expert* (1952), *Waiting for the Mahatma* (1955), *The Man-Eater of Malgudi* (1961), *The Vendor of Sweets* (1967), *The Painter of Signs* (1977), *A Tiger for Malgudi* (1983) and *Talkative Man* (1986). His novel *The Guide* (1958) won him the National Prize of the Indian Literary Academy, his country's highest literary honour. As well as five collections of short stories, *A Horse and Two Goats*, *An Astrologer's Day and Other Stories*, *Lawley Road*, *Malgudi Days* and *Under the Banyan Tree*, he has published two travel books, *My Dateless Diary* and *The Emerald Route*; four volumes of essays, *Next Saturday*, *Reluctant Guru*, *A Story-teller's World* and *A Writer's Nightmare*; the retold legends, *Gods, Demons and Others*, *The Ramayana* and *The Mahabharata*; and a volume of memoirs, *My Days*. In 1980 he was awarded the A. C. Benson Medal by the Royal Society of Literature and in 1982 he was made an Honorary Member of the American Academy and Institute of Arts and Letters. Many of his books are published by Penguin.

R. K. Narayan

THE PAINTER OF SIGNS

PENGUIN BOOKS

PENGUIN BOOKS

Published by the Penguin Group
Penguin Books Ltd, 27 Wrights Lane, London W8 5TZ, England
Penguin Books USA Inc., 375 Hudson Street, New York, New York 10014, USA
Penguin Books Australia Ltd, Ringwood, Victoria, Australia
Penguin Books Canada Ltd, 10 Alcorn Avenue, Toronto, Ontario, Canada M4V 3B2
Penguin Books (NZ) Ltd, 182–190 Wairau Road, Auckland 10, New Zealand

Penguin Books Ltd, Registered Offices: Harmondsworth, Middlesex, England

First published in the USA by The Viking Press 1976
First published in Canada by The Macmillan Company of Canada Ltd 1976
First published in Great Britain by William Heinemann Ltd 1977
Published in Penguin Books 1982
9 10

Printed in England by Clays Ltd, St Ives plc
Set in VIP Baskerville

Part One

Raman's was the last house in Ellaman Street; a little door on the back wall opened, beyond a stretch of sand, to the river. He would lay out a plank of wood brushed over with black or white base and leave it out to dry, on the sand. This was a fairly untroubled work spot, the granite steps where bathers congregated being further down the river; but for some goatherd who might peep over the wall, no one disturbed his peace; occasionally, however, if he was careless, a strong breeze blowing from the river sprayed sand particles on his wet board. He had had trouble, a couple of months before, with a lawyer who was setting up his office in Kabir Street, and who had ordered his nameboard to be delivered on a certain auspicious day.

Earlier, Raman had been button-holed by the lawyer at the market gate.

'The very man I was looking for,' said the lawyer, holding him up. He had undergone a correspondence course in law. 'I must give you the happy news just received: I have passed the law, and I want your help to get my nameboard done immediately.'

'Certainly, I'm at your service,' said Raman.

'I knew you would help me,' said the lawyer. 'I want it before eleven a.m. on Thursday.'

'Impossible,' said Raman. 'I want at least five days – drying takes time . . .' He felt desperate, having to explain to man after man how one had to allow time for paint to dry. No one understood the importance of this.

The lawyer said, 'Come on, let us have coffee. I must explain.' They were jostled by the evening crowd at the market gate. Pushing his bicycle along, Raman followed him into the restaurant across the street, from where emanated not only the flavour of frying oil but also loud film music from a radio fixed to the wall. They sat at a table. The lawyer beckoned to a boy who was darting about the tables, and bawled his order over the din of clattering cups and film music. Sipping coffee, the prospective lawyer said, 'I must have the board absolutely on Thursday before eleven. I should not miss that time.'

'Why not?' Raman asked.

'My astrologer says so. Please, you must . . .' He leaned forward and shouted over the noise, 'I am not taking a refusal from you. What'll you charge?'

'Thirty rupees for three lines minimum, one three-by-one-and-a-half plank, including nailing.'

'Show some concession, please. I'm just starting on my career.'

'Materials alone will cost about eighteen rupees –' began Raman.

'I like the letters to be slanted a little,' the lawyer said.

Here is the fellow, with nothing settled but talks of style, thought Raman. 'Impossible,' he cried, having his own notions of calligraphy suitable for a lawyer. 'Slanting letters are suitable only for oil-merchants and soap-sellers.'

The lawyer became insistent. Raman tried to explain his philosophy of calligraphy. 'Sir, listen to me. The letters on a lawyer's board must always stand up proudly, and not lie supine. Head erect.' The man repeated his specification. Raman felt that he needed enlightenment and launched on fierce dialectics; persons seated at other tables suspended their own arguments to watch the fun here.

'You are going to be a lawyer, not a kerosene-merchant,' said Raman.

The other replied, undaunted, 'I want the letters to be slanted, to the left – otherwise it will be of no use to me.'

Raman's curiosity got the better of him, and he asked, 'What makes you so firm?'

'It's my astrologer again, who believes that a left slant is auspicious for my ruling star, which is Saturn.'

Raman was upset. All day long he was engaged in arguing with his old aunt who advised him to do this or that according to the stars. He was determined to establish the Age of Reason in the world. 'I want a rational explanation for everything,' he cried. 'Otherwise my mind refuses to accept any statement.' He was bursting with self-declarations. 'I'm a rationalist, and I don't do anything unless I see some logic in it.'

The lawyer, born to controvert all statements, said, 'What more logic do you want than that I'm paying for it? And I want it that way and the slanting letters to be shaded; that's all there is to it. What more do you want than that?'

'That sounds pretty convincing,' Raman cried, holding out his hand. 'Don't forget that no money has passed yet, and the command is premature.' The lawyer dramatically pulled out his purse and gave him a ten-rupee note. Raman said, 'Make it twenty. I have to buy the wooden plank and paint. You may pay the balance on delivery.'

'On Thursday before eleven,' emphasized the man once more, and they rose to leave. Before they parted at the junction of Kabir Street, Raman asked again, 'So you don't mind the oil-monger style?'

'I go by what my astrologer says,' said the lawyer. 'Saves a lot of trouble that way.'

'I prefer to think for myself,' Raman said before turning his cycle round homeward. 'All our great minds, from Valluvar down to Bernard Shaw and Einstein, say . . .'

'Say what?' asked the lawyer, pausing.

'I couldn't quote,' Raman said, 'even if I were the author of those sentiments, but I'll copy them down for you some day.'

'Before eleven on Thursday, at least half an hour before. Must have time to fix it on the wall.'

Raman worked feverishly until late on Wednesday night, and on Thursday he cycled up to Kabir Street carrying the sign-board in a wrapping, tied to the cycle cross-bar. The lawyer had given a grand setting to his inauguration, with his threshold strung with mango leaves. Only a pipe and band and a bride missing to make it a wedding celebration, Raman reflected.

The lawyer had invited some guests, who were being received by his aged father and seated on a carpet in the passage amidst incense, holy fire, and a lot of chanting by a group of priests. The scent of jasmine pervaded the air. Numerous children chased each other about noisily. The lawyer himself was in a state of holiness, draped in red silk, forehead blazoned with vermilion and sandal paste. He had gone hoarse reciting holy verse all through the morning. Raman leaned his bicycle on the lamp-post beside the gutter in front of the house and was locking up its wheels when someone from within the house cried, 'No need to lock the cycle, we are all here . . .'

What if you are there? commented Raman inaudibly. Who are you? How do I know that you won't steal the cycle yourself? He inserted the chain between the spokes and clicked the lock, saying to himself, Now this is better. If a chap wants to steal, he will have to carry the bicycle on his head because the wheels won't roll now. He untied the sign-board from the cross-bar of his bicycle and carried it in delicately. At the sight of him several people cried, 'The board has come, the board has come!'

'Leave way!' shouted the lawyer, who became excited at the sight of it.

Raman pointed triumphantly at the hands of his wrist watch. 'Ten-thirty means ten-thirty in my dictionary.'

'I was anxious whether it'd come in time, if it had been late . . .'

A tufted priest came up to remark, 'The essence lies in correct timing, a minute this way or that can make all the difference between a millionaire and a mendicant.'

'Be scientific, please, scientific,' Raman tried to say, but felt distracted when several hands reached for the board. He held off, warning everyone, 'Not yet, not yet. Still not dry. The letter "A" with all that amount of shading on its side will take time to dry. Don't touch "A" whatever you may do.' He held up the plank, lifting a corner of the plastic wrap to afford a glimpse of the writing on it to the lawyer.

'Ah!' cried the lawyer, 'I hope it's perfect. That slant, I mean.'

Raman spurned the man's anxiety about the angle of the letters and his esoteric theories, and merely said, 'You will not miss anything you have asked for. Let me first nail it up properly. Tell me where you want it.'

'I have kept some nails –' began the lawyer.

'Keep them,' said Raman. 'I provide the nails and also the services of a hammer for hitting them on the head.' He indicated a bag, slung on his shoulder, with the bust of Gandhi printed in green dye on it. He found himself surrounded by an admiring crowd. They'll probably ask for my autograph soon, Raman thought. Why should they gape at me like this? Nothing else to do . . . hundreds and thousands of people in this town have nothing better to do than watch, watch, watch and gape, all day.

The parched old man, the lawyer's father, said over the babble, 'You may start nailing up in a quarter of an hour.' The lawyer and his two cousins became suddenly very active and effusive, and gently propelled Raman towards the kitchen, saying, 'Coffee and *idli* for this man.' They shouted, '*Idli* for one,' into the kitchen. A group of little boys and girls followed him wherever he went. Out of the smoke-filled kitchen, a woman emerged blowing her nose and wiping her eyes, bearing on a little banana leaf two white *idlis*, tinted with red chilli-powder and oil; at the sight of this, Raman felt hungry. He had had no respite since the morning to think of breakfast, although his old aunt had gone on inquiring from her kitchen, 'What do you like to have? You have eaten nothing today.' He had ignored her, as he had to concentrate on the finishing of the board. Now, he carefully placed the board against the wall, ate the two *idlis*, and after washing them down with coffee served in a brass cup, felt revived, though he felt like announcing, This coffee is too dilute. Not the way it should be made. Anyway, you give it at a scalding temperature, which benumbs the tongue and one can't notice what one is consuming. But your *idli* is light and up to the mark, thank you all.

Every little movement of his and every word that he uttered were being watched by a zealous crowd; he only hoped that they would not read his thoughts. He was aware that he had of late got into the habit of communicating on two planes – audibly and inaudibly at the same time. Through the open roof of the courtyard, smoke from the holy fire was escaping with the unholy fire from the kitchen. Raman thought, They are blinding that poor lady, whoever she may be, who is manufacturing the *idlis* in that black hole of a kitchen. A row of crows sat on the parapet waiting to dive at any edible within sight. Children kept up an unvarying noise level. The heat and congestion were oppressive, and Raman wished he could flee, leaving the nailing to others. But that would be against his professional practice. He liked to hang up a sign properly. He thought, Some people are so dense that they might hang a thing upside down and then blame the sign-board painter for writing the letters upside down!

The parched old man came up to him with the chief priest, ordered the children, 'Get out of the way, brats.' He was getting excited at the approach of the auspicious moment. Raman briskly got up and followed the old man out. He said, 'This is where it must be,' pointing at an outer wall. Raman now unwound the wrapping, held the board against the wall, made a pencil mark, and plied the hammer. He ignored the assembly, and the street-hawkers and passersby who paused to watch the proceedings. The priest stretched a jasmine garland across the board, touched it with sandal paste, recited something aloud, commanding the lawyer to repeat after him, circled a camphor, and sounded a bell all at once. Several women emerged from various corners of the house and congratulated the new lawyer. All this was staged on a narrow space between the wall of the house and the edge of a gutter.

Tears filled the eyes of the parched old man. 'We come of a family of judges and lawyers. That's why I was so keen my son should become a lawyer. Now these are not outsiders or guests – but members of my own family. We are six brothers, and these are nephews and grandchildren.'

Someone turned on gramophone music inside that congested house. A note of discord was struck when the lawyer suddenly said after touching the surface of the board, 'What's this? Dirt? Am I to start my career with dirt on my name?' Raman looked puzzled, and then felt panicky at the sudden threat of a crisis. He wanted to remain non-committal as long as possible and for a moment wished he could hop on his bicycle and run away. The crowd became silent, just waiting to see what interesting developments would follow. Meanwhile the lawyer had taken hold of Raman's hand and was navigating him closer to the board. Raman snapped his hand free as if he were being asked to touch fire and cried, 'Careful! Four "A"s are still wet. You don't want them to become smears, do you? Thank God you are not a barrister-at-law, otherwise there would have been three more "A"s, and with your passion for slanting and shading the stroke we'd never have got anywhere with this programme.'

The auspicious plans seemed to have suddenly come to a halt. Even the gramophone inside ceased, and a bunch of young men, students of the local college, admirers of hippie philosophies, as evident from their side-burns and check shirts, came out to see what was going on, adding to the circle of watchers. Arguments were proceeding apace. The lawyer asked, 'Do you want me to start my career with dirt on my name?'

You are bound to have it sooner or later, why not now? But aloud Raman said with a forced laugh, running his finger over the surface of the board, 'Oh! This is not dirt, only river sand, to give it a stucco effect.'

'What's stucco?' asked the lawyer challengingly.

A hippie-like youth came out to explain, 'Don't you know, uncle? Latest in architectural surfaces.' He was a student of engineering.

Bless your enlightened mind. May your side-burns flourish! thought Raman. Nodding a thanks to the fellow, 'You look like Robert Louis Stevenson, Faraday, and a host of other celebrities to be seen only in our ancient schoolbooks.'

'I never asked for it,' said the lawyer. 'I don't want to pay for a lot of sand on my first board.' Raman understood how it must have happened. While giving the final touches to the board at his back yard, he had felt cool and grateful for a sudden gust of wind from the river, but it had brought along a minute pinch of sand and scattered it all over the wet white base.

A sudden sense of fair play seized Raman, and he said, 'I'll write another one for you. Keep this one for the day, because you should not miss the good time.' The tension in the air suddenly relaxed. People stirred on the margin of the gutter and made way for Raman to move.

The old father came up with the chief priest and said, 'Yes, that's what I also wanted to suggest; but after all we are old-fashioned, and I don't know modern fashions. Yes, what's done is God's will and we must leave it alone.'

'But I will replace it soon,' said Raman, fumbling for his cycle-key.

The lawyer said, 'Of course, that's all right. But don't go away yet.' He commanded one of his nephews, 'Give him coconut and leaves.' They brought a pink paper bag stuffed with a coconut and betel leaves and held it out to him, which meant that the honoured guest could now depart.

This Kabir Street is choking, he said to himself. How do people live here? He bicycled along and, at the intersection of Market Road, paused to consider what he should do next. Without dismounting, he rested his feet on a wayside culvert and asked himself, Where shall I go? He had spent two hours in the lawyer's house. Nearing one o'clock in the afternoon. He realized that he had not been paid for his labour, and, technically speaking, the day had been wasted. He should be throwing good money after bad money if he tried to do another board for the lawyer. The plank had cost four rupees and a new brush one rupee and paint one rupee. The lawyer had paid him ten, and so he still had his margin.

His reverie ended when a policeman on traffic duty at the fountain blew his whistle and gestured to him to move on. When Raman failed to obey, he blew his whistle again and flourished his arms wildly. Raman felt, They won't leave one in peace. This is a jungle where other beasts are constantly on the prowl to attack and bite off a mouthful, if one is not careful. As if this were New York and I blocked the traffic on Broadway. He would not recognize it, but Malgudi was changing in 1972. It was the base for a hydro-electric project somewhere on the Mempi Hills, and jeeps and lorries passed through the Market Road all day. The city had a new superintendent of police who was trying out new ideas. Policemen were posted every few yards. They seem to be excited at the spectacle of all this traffic, he thought, imagining that we are on the verge of disaster, I suppose, with pedestrians and vehicles bumping into each other.

When the policeman blew his whistle for the third time, he moved on slowly. They won't give me time to think what I should do next, he said to himself. It'd have saved me a lot of worry if that lawyer had asked me to stay on to lunch. They were preparing a feast, I noticed, but that niggard disposed of me with two *idlis* and a coconut and no money.

If the lawyer had given him the fee for the board, he might have eaten at Anand Bhavan, where one got a sort of Bombay food, but now one had to go home, or try a place in Ellaman Street known as The Boardless Hotel, run by a man who capitalized on the fact that he had no name for his restaurant, which made it attractive to a certain type of custom. 'Can I do you a "nameless" board?' Raman often quipped. He speculated sometimes what he would do for a living if everyone adopted the boardless notion. They might engage him to inscribe gossip or blackmail on public walls; do it on the command of one and rub it off on the command of another. Sivanand, the municipal chairman, would provide enough material for all the blank walls of the city. His enemies could offer five rupees a line for writing, and Sivanand's supporters ten rupees for rubbing it off. A better medium than a scandal-sheet, less perishable. You could have a new item each day about this or that man, the renting of market stalls, the contract for that piece of roadmending, change of name in order to immortalize a visiting minister and gain his favour; and a thousand other sins. What about the American milk powder meant for the orphans of India and sold on the black market? What about the government hospital surgeon who flourished his knife like an assassin and made money and acquired the much-coveted building sites beyond the railway crossing! And that wholesale grain-merchant who cornered all the rationed articles and ran the co-operative stores meant for the poor? Raman would expose them to the world if someone paid him and provided him with a spacious wall, but ironically enough, he wrote sign-boards for most of them. A sign-board was inevitable in modern life, a token of respectable and even noble intentions. But he felt abashed when he realized that he was perhaps picking his own loot in the general scramble of a money-mad world! He wished he could do without it, but realized too that it was like a desire for a dry spot while drifting along neck deep in a cesspool. Ultimately he would evolve a scheme for doing without money. While bicycling, his mind attained a certain passivity, and ideas bubbled up, lingered a while, burst, and vanished.

He went home, and straight on to his room, where he peeled off his shirt and vest, which had become sticky on this hot day. He opened the door at the back yard, passed swiftly across the sands to the river-steps, and dipped himself in the water. Felt refreshed. He noticed a woman standing knee deep in water, with her sari tucked up, washing clothes. He stepped further down until the water reached up to his chin, bowed his head, and plunged in for a brief moment, seeing nothing, hearing nothing, suffocating pleasantly with water shooting up his nostrils; even the rustle of leaves from the tall peepul trees was unheard for a while. When he emerged on the surface and opened his eyes, he noticed the woman's thigh. Nice sight, he told himself, Thigh fairer than her face, naturally. He lingered on the spectacle for a little while, checked his thoughts as being unholy, averted his head, and hurried back home. Living on the river, he occasionally entertained himself by watching the bathers, and was fairly accustomed to the sight of the human figure in the wet; but it always ended in self-criticism. He wanted to get away from sex thoughts, minimize their importance, just as he wished to reduce the importance of money. Money and sex, he reflected, obsessive thoughts, too much everywhere – literature, magazines, drama, or cinema deal with nothing but sex all the time, but the female figure, water-soaked, is enchanting.

He had come back to his room, dried himself, and changed his clothes. His aunt, who had dozed off in her corner, now woke up to inquire, 'I saw you bathe at the well this morning, why again at the river?' He felt slightly irritated. Why should she bother about his bathing habits? She concluded, 'Take care, you may catch a cold.'

He spurned her advice and asked, 'Have you eaten?'

'Today I fast,' she said. Her fortnightly day of fasting. He didn't like to announce that he had not eaten. He looked at himself in the mirror, combing his hair, as his comb splashed off water-drops from his hair. Must write a poem or something, he thought, about a man who looked into a mirror for the first time and collapsed with a groan. But I'm not so bad. One has to get used to appearances, I suppose. A question of usage.

'What was the feast like?' she asked from her corner. He had told her in the morning that he was likely to eat at the lawyer's.

'As usual,' he said, avoiding the truth. He reflected, Truth? On three occasions, you need not speak the truth. To save a life, to save an honour . . . and the third I can't remember, but I suppose to save an aunt the bother of cooking for you.

He quickly left, to lunch at The Boardless Hotel.

Occupying his usual corner at the back of the smoky hall, he ate off a banana leaf spread out on a greasy teak-wood table, uttering pleasantries to a group of habitual fellow-lunchers, the most vociferous in the company being Gupta, who was always incensed over government policies at every level, city, state, national, and international, and who anticipated disaster every morrow. Raman, of course, did not think that Gupta's comments were worth hearing. But Gupta gave him much work, as he started a new business under a new name each year in order to confound the sales tax, income tax, and all other governmental tax-devisers. Establishing a new enterprise meant only blacking out an old sign and writing a new one in its place, and he paid down five rupees per letter without a word. And he appreciated anyone who refrained from contradicting his political views. He ate every day at the same hour at The Boardless Hotel. 'Indira Gandhi is dynamic, no doubt, but I do not approve of –' it could be nationalization of banks, export policy, or anything.

'Yes, yes,' murmured Raman, while at the back of his mind he regretted that he had hurried away from the river-steps instead of observing the woman fully.

'Or take the question of national integration. I'm a Gupta and you are a Raman, from different ends of the country. Yet I do my business here, and you do your business here . . . do you ask a question?'

'No,' said Raman weakly, and added emphatically, 'of course not. Why should I?' while mentally he completed the sentence with the inquiry, The girl at the river – was she a girl or lady or woman or just a female? Was she stocky, tall, fair, or ugly? Nothing noted. The glimpse of the thigh below the hem of her tucked-up sari had monopolized his attention, and then the quick and desperate effort to get away from the resulting sequence of thoughts, imagery, and wishful speculations: Why did I run away from the steps? Just my principle, and disciplining my mind against sex – obsessive sex.

They had now reached the end of the meal. Buttermilk had been served. Gupta moved on to the wash-basin to clean his fingers and rinse his mouth noisily. Raman went to another wash-basin and left. On his way out, he picked up a pan from the table of the proprietor, who was waiting to collect the bills, and passed out of the door saying, 'Put it down in my account,' with the usual joke, 'and keep it there until you decide to hang a sign-board to say "Boardless" on your door, which will settle our accounts.' He had left Gupta somewhere at the rear part of the hall in semi-darkness. Good chap, never expected you to stay on for him to finish his speech.

Raman crossed the street and was back in his house. Aunt had not bolted the door, and he was able to slip in and pass into his room without rousing her. He felt relieved that he could achieve it – as he always found her either asking questions or narrating a story or reminiscing. His room was without table or chair. He had a mat and a roll of bedding; when he wished to sleep, he unrolled the bed, but when he wanted to read, he sat reclining on the rolled-up bed, lost in the pages of some ancient volume. His cupboard overflowed with the books he had cherished since his college days – Plato to *Pickwick Papers*, some of them in double-column editions, with paper turning grey, yellow, and brown and etchings that transported him. He knew a second-hand bookseller at the market who gathered books from far and wide. Raman's great delight in life was to pick up a bargain at the antiquarian shop. He wrote the bookseller's sign-board for him and burnished it anew from time to time, and picked up a book or two instead of presenting a bill. He was fascinated by that man, as he had absolutely no customers coming into his shop, and what sustained him was his acceptance of failure. A pessimist revelling in pessimism, and gloating over his frustrations, with all kinds of books heaped around him. The patterns and designs that book-worms created on the book-covers and insides made him ecstatic. He spent his hours studying them and discussing them with Raman. 'Book-worms possess a sense of design,' he would explain. 'Some books are tunnelled end to end, some they give up with the preface, in some they create a perfect wizardry of design but confined to the end-papers, never an inch beyond. A real masterpiece must be read only in an ancient edition and you could easily recognize it by the fact that the book-worm has already gone through it end to end and left its testimonial in its own code.'

For browsing in the afternoon Raman hardly cared what book he chose; it might be Gibbon's *Decline and Fall* or *Kural* – that tenth-century Tamil classic. He had a general philosophy of books – all the classification that mattered was good books and bad books, and the antiquarian could be depended upon not to nurture bad books. Raman's practice was to put his hand into the cupboard and take out the first book that his finger touched. Before settling down, he shut his door so that he might not be disturbed either by his aunt or her afternoon visitors, who generally dropped in to seek her advice on some domestic matters, listen to her discourse on the gods, swallow some herbal remedy, or listen to her prophecies from a horoscope. Raman was so used to her that he hardly ever noticed how very versatile she was. Everyone who came across her was wonder-struck at the variety of her accomplishments. But Raman was indifferent, and could never get over a feeling that she was somewhat bogus.

Whenever Raman's aunt could catch his attention, mostly when serving food, she spoke non-stop and punctuated her statements with, 'If you write my life, you will be producing a masterpiece, which people will read and enjoy.' He generally listened to her passively. But one day, provoked by her challenge, 'If you write my story, you will make more money than you do now writing sign-boards for all the merchants of the town,' he answered back, 'I write not for merchants alone, but also for lawyers, doctors, and govern-ment officers.'

'Maybe, but if you write my story, you may throw away your brush forever. So many persons come and listen to my narrative every day!' She had sounded so eager to dictate her story that, after finishing his dinner, he went to his room, came back to her with a pad and pencil, and said, 'Now come on, what's your story?'

She was cleaning up after the dinner. 'Wait,' she said, as he stood behind her with his pencil poised theatrically. She went on scrubbing the kitchen floor with a short broom; to the accompaniment of its continuous scratching sound, she said, 'Remember I was not always seventy-five or eighty years old. There was a time when I was just ten years old. You write that down first.'

Raman made a note of it and looked up: 'What next?'

'Read it aloud,' she said. And he repeated, 'I was not born seventy-five or eighty years old.'

She continued, 'When I was ten years old, I remember clearly that I could just reach up to a mirror hung on the wall in our home, to arrange my hair, which was wavy and streamed down to my hips. People came and admired me in those days.'

Raman proceeded to take it down, pausing to throw a brief glance at her head, now covered with a thin layer of milk-white hair gathered into a small knot at the back. She followed his look and patted her head, halting the scratchy broom for a moment. 'You don't believe me? Surely. In those days no photography was known . . . Otherwise . . .' She did not finish her sentence. He studied her. Impossible to connect this frail, shrinking, wrinkled personality with her own description of herself. She continued her narrative. 'I was one of the several children in the house. It's not like these days when people are afraid of children. The house was full in those days. But nothing bothered anyone in those days – as long as there was a well-stocked granary and the bronze rice-pot was on the boil. My father was a priest and officiated at birthdays, funerals, and all kinds of religious functions and brought home his fee in the form of rice and vegetables and coconut and sugar-cane. Occasionally he also brought in a cow, which, as you know, when gifted to a brahmin helps a dead man's soul to ford a difficult river in the next world.'

'How?' questioned the rationalist.

'Don't ask me all that,' Aunt said. 'That's what our shastras say, and we don't have to question it. It is the duty of the living to help the dead with proper rituals,' Raman felt irritated at her beliefs. How could the Age of Reason be established if people were like this! Impossible.

He said, 'All right, go on with your story.'

'We were a well-fed lot in our home. I was especially fortunate as I had the name of the Goddess of Wealth, Laxmi, and no one dared say, "Go away, Laxmi," as it might be inauspicious. It was always good to say, "Oh, Laxmi, welcome to our house," and I was invited ungrudgingly into any of the hundred houses in our village. I was pampered wherever I went, and grew fat.'

'Where is all that fat gone now?' asked Raman.

The old lady had by now finished her work, laid away the broom and vessels, and said, 'One cannot forever flourish and fatten in a father's house, especially one born woman.' She dictated up to the stage where she married a head constable in a near-by village and his untimely death which left her barren and widowed.

This afternoon Raman's fingers had picked up a gilt-edged worm-eaten book of reminiscences by an early teaplanter who had had his estate on the Mempi Hills over a hundred years before. The planter had come all the way from Cornwall and spent a lifetime in the misty hills of Mempi range cultivating tea and surviving with the help of a double-barrelled gun and a devil-may-care attitude. Raman was lost in visions and dreams of those misty ranges, the dripping plantations in monsoon, the tigers and elephants warded off with gunfire, and the social background of a remote world consisting of a colony of estate workers dominated by an English planter with his nearest neighbour, another planter, fifty miles away. Raman said to himself, Must retire on an estate when all the sign-boards of this city are finished . . . and dozed off with the book on his chest. He woke up when the fat volume slipped down to the floor with a thud, and immediately thought, Must get the money from the bangle-seller. After six, the fellow will be gone. Have to buy a new brush with the money. The one in use has begun to scratch the board.

Sound of unlocking the cycle roused his aunt's attention. 'Already leaving, why?'

He mumbled some reply in slight irritation. Wants to know everything, he thought, took his cycle down the steps and was off before the old lady could come out and ask more questions. He entered the market by its western gate, wishing to avoid Jayaraj at the other gate, who fancied himself a sign-board painter. Illiterate fellow (had no elementary notion of length – his own sign-board jutted out of the wall, blocking half the way), but he snatched up a lot of orders and – subleasing the job – got them written by Antony, who was grateful to be paid twenty paisa per letter. This business was sinking to mean levels, with illiterates, possessing no feeling for calligraphy, handling it. If this continued, he'd abandon the town and look for a career on a tea estate, live in a hut, and watch the horizon at off-hours.

The bangle-seller's shop, that single cubicle beyond the banana godown, was crowded with women bargaining, chattering, selecting and changing their selections, and thrusting up their wrists for more bangles. The bangle-seller was continuously squeezing wrists while slipping on the bangles. Pleasantest job, Raman reflected. He noticed that the sign-board he had delivered on the previous day was still in a corner within its paper wrapper. Evidently the man had been holding hands continuously and could not find a free moment. The lecher! Raman picked up the board and held it aloft for him to see. Some schoolgirls read it out and giggled. STRICTLY CASH said the sign, in fiery, glowing colours, 'Cash' particularly had the appearance of live charcoal.

This place smells too womanly – perfume, talcum, hair-oil, perspiration – suits that lecher perhaps, but not me, reflected Raman.

The bangle-seller looked up from a wrist without letting it go and said, ' "Cash" is too red . . . It'll put people off.'

'But that's how you wanted it.'

The bangle-seller did not answer this point but concentrated his attention on a plump wrist – massaging it down to suit the circumstance of a bangle. The woman enjoyed it and moaned with delicious pain. Raman watched the scene for some moments and commented within himself: Dalliance and flirtation. I now realize why this chap is persisting in this fragile trade – if a couple of well-aimed pebbles are flung into the shop he will be ruined. Why don't you employ a couple of girls for this job, leaving yourself free to discuss business with sign-board painters?

It was difficult to get in a word with this man, and Raman felt irritated and humiliated. 'Why don't you pay my bill? You asked me to come for it today,' he said over the babble and the squealings of women.

'I don't like the red in "cash"; you must change it.'

'But you wanted it that way.'

'Not so red. My customers won't like it.' He turned to a girl waiting to be attended and asked, 'Do you like that?' She giggled, turned away her head, and shook with laughter. He urged, 'Come on, say what you have on your mind.' The village girl murmured coyly, 'I like only blue colour.'

Very attractive, seductive scene, but no money in it for me, Raman reflected. At the same moment, he was seized with a ridiculous feeling, holding up his handiwork for all to see, as if he were auctioning his sign-board to a set of ecstatic females.

'Why is your shop so crowded today?' he could not help asking.

The man replied, 'This is the season. Pongal coming, it's auspicious for women to renew their bangles. They come from far and near. They know they'll have the best selections here – both glass and plastic,' and he looked around beamingly for approval.

Raman asked curtly, 'Are you paying me now or not?'

'Yes, if you change that colour to blue.'

'Don't you understand that if you want strict cash dealing in your shop and "cash" in blue, people may laugh at you? They won't take you seriously. Now in the present colour, they can't escape, they can't miss your idea. I can't write a new board.' The bangle-seller was unmoved. It looked as though the man were backing out. 'If you don't want it, why did you order this board?' There was no answer. The man let go a slender wrist and stood up menacingly. He wanted to show off as a hero before his admiring customers. Raman was surprised at the turn of events, and backed away slightly. The man looked muscular. Raman said, 'If you don't want it, you don't want, that's all,' and quietly retreated from the shop with the sign-board under his arm.

Made a mistake in accepting this custom, he said to himself. He took his cycle off its stand at the western arch of the market with his mind preoccupied. Three days' labour lost . . . and that lawyer! Sometimes it's a bad day all through in every way.

Market Road was crowded and active as ever. This was the hour at which the goods train arrived, and all kinds of barrels, packages, and bags were unloaded at the railway station, and then piled up on the bullock-carts, which lumbered along to the godowns behind the market. As he cycled down avoiding the country carts, Raman wondered for a moment whether he should not try and sell the board to some other shopkeeper. This sign-board, with its flaming injunction to pay cash, should appeal to anyone. He saw the owner of Bhandari Stores standing at his door, and slowed down. A wafer-thin man with a waxed moustache so finely pointed and turned parallel to the earth that if you stepped too close it might puncture your eyes, who claimed to have come down from Rajasthan and settled here many generations ago, and was a good friend, speaking a sort of quaint Tamil which generally fascinated Raman. The man hailed him and asked, 'Busy day?'

'Yes, of course,' Raman said, hopping off his saddle. He went into the shop and held up the sign-board. 'How do you like this?' he asked.

The businessman became cautious and said, 'No business for me unless I give credit. God knows what trouble it is getting back my money.'

'You must sell strictly for cash,' Raman repeated, the flaming message drumming in his brain.

'I wish I could,' said the man, 'but that will be possible only in the next world.'

Raman understood it'd be no use canvassing here, and bantered, 'Shall I add "also for credit" in green letters? That might please the customers.'

The man catching only the word 'green' and paying no attention to the rest of the sentence replied, 'Green will be better.' He took a second look at the sign-board and said, 'This red is too much, sir. The customer must not feel upset.'

Raman suppressed all the offensive remarks that came to his head. People really needed to be educated in good taste. The man asked for green. Green! Good heavens, what was the world coming to! He feared that he might get into a fight if he stayed longer, mumbled a farewell, pushed off his bicycle, and was gone, with his mind in a turmoil. A number of things upset him – not the least of them being the thought that the world was peopled by persons who expected 'cash' to be written in green. The fault is in the educational system and the political leadership, people who ought to mould the taste of the public and help their minds to grow were busy otherwise.

He passed the town hall building. Noticed the fountain spraying up water today – rather a rare sight. He bicycled down the drive, leaned his cycle on the parapet, and stooped to splash cold water on his fevered brow, tucking the sign-board under his arm. Turning round, he noticed the Town Hall Professor (a local eccentric who appeared at the town hall fountain every evening, clad in a purple academic gown and harangued the public on a variety of matters), sitting cross-legged on the parapet, delivering a spiritual message to a small circle of listeners. He was saying, 'Past is gone, present is going, and tomorrow is day after tomorrow's yesterday. So why worry about anything? God is in all this. He is one and indivisible. He is in yesterday, tomorrow, and today. If you think it over properly, you will never sigh for anything coming or going.' He held up a small slip of paper, folded and gummed, and said, 'Here is the message that will help you. This will cost you five paisa. Take it home and read it and your mind will be cleansed and illuminated. I'd give it away free, but I have to recover the actual cost.' A few persons came forward, gave him the money and bought the message. The Professor said, 'Open it only in your home, before the gods in the puja room, and follow the injunction in it.' He suddenly said to his audience, 'See the message this young man is carrying – "Strictly Cash" – a message for the money-mad world. What is cash? What is strict?'

Raman felt self-conscious and in his clumsiness held up the board for all to see. People studied it seriously and a general murmur broke out – all kinds of comments. Rather irritated, Raman asked, 'Does anyone want it? Fifteen rupees.' He somehow felt that he was taking it out on the original bangle-seller by offering this to the public.

The Professor said, 'No credit. Strictly, strictly, strictly, cash, cash, cash! That is what the world is coming to.'

Everyone looked at Raman jeeringly. He hated to have become the butt of all this jocularity. 'What's wrong with it? How can we live without cash? How can we? How?'

He could hardly be heard. They kept commenting in a jumble. 'Don't argue with the learned man. Are you wiser than he?'

'He is also giving it not free, but only for cash,' said Raman.

'That's true,' murmured a group in support of him.

The Professor was nonplussed only for a moment, but said smartly 'This is just nominal. Five paisa for such a profound message!'

'Why don't you hang this on this parapet?' asked Raman cynically.

'Yes, why not?' said the Professor. He snatched it from Raman, leaned it against the fountain wall, and said, 'I'll take this as your payment.' He held out the packet. 'Take it home and follow the advice in it, you will be all the better for it. You will find a change in your life.' The transaction was too far gone for Raman to withdraw his offer. He brooded for a moment. He was amused at the thought that this sign-board was after all destined to decorate the town hall fountain. While he was lost in reflection, holding in his palm the piece of paper, the Professor went on repeating, 'Yesterday was yesterday. Here is the solution to all your problems.'

A drunkard elbowed his way through demanding to know what the packet contained. 'Don't think I am drunk. I know what's what. You must tell me, great one! What does it contain? I never buy anything I don't want to buy anything I don't . . . who can challenge me? Who saw me drink? Let every true son of his true father prove it. Is it your grandfather's property? I say what I tell them . . .' He stood lightly rocking until the others pushed him aside and came forward to take the message. Raman felt it'd be useless to stay any longer. There was no chance of any improvement in the deal with the Professor. He abruptly withdrew and cycled homeward.

Reaching his room, he unfolded the piece of paper containing the Town Hall Professor's message. On a ribbon-wide strip, it was written '*This will pass*,' in three languages in addition to English. Four lines of minute writing in black ink; Raman admired the calligraphy. I must try to learn more about this calligraphist, he resolved. Will be more worth while than writing sign-boards for rascally bangle-sellers. He studied the message, and its significance seemed to deepen while he brooded over it, giving him a feeling of perpetually gliding away from objects and moments. Losing all sense of stagnation, Raman felt suddenly light at heart.

Raman could hear the sound of the grindstone coming from the back yard. Aunt must be busy making something, he thought, some flour, the first stage in planning some delicacy for the morrow. He felt a stab of sympathy for her. Morning till night, planning something for his delectation – for years, unwavering attention to his needs. She rarely asked him for anything in return, no demands whatever, went up to the store for replenishment of groceries. The Chettiar shop was her farthest horizon, westward at the corner of Ellaman Street and Market Road. The shopman sat in the midst of an array of sacks of rice and corn and a variety of sundries in little tin containers and bottles. His principle was to be able to say, 'Yes, I have it,' and pick up in that cavernous hall whatever a customer might ask for. If he did not have it, he'd always say, 'I'm expecting a supply tomorrow. Come at about this time . . .' He had a philosophy that the Goddess of Wealth spurned a trader who gave a negative answer. His shop was in two halves – one contained the normal requirements of his customers, such as rice and pulses; and the other, inner one was stocked with an odd assortment – over one thousand different categories. 'If someone wants an inch-square of the sole of a worn-out shoe, I'll have it, or a rusty nail, or a clipping of the hair on a cat's tail – I keep everything in stock, labelled and preserved. Sometimes people come to me with strange demands while attempting to make their own medicines, fumigations, or talismans, and I supply whatever they may want, never turning away anyone,' he told Raman five years ago, when he had gone up to deliver his sign-board, one of his earliest professional engagements. The man wanted nothing more than CHETTIAR STORES – just one line on a small plank. All the white lettering was now faded and the black base was dust-covered, hardly distinguishable from the wall on which it was nailed. While bicycling up the street it hurt Raman's eyes, and once he stopped to ask, 'Why don't I clean up and rewrite that sign?' But the man was satisfied with the griminess of things. 'No need to announce myself – my customers know it, and will always come to this Chettiar,' he had said. His bare body merged with the dark interior of his shop. There was a rock-like permanence about the things there. Nothing changed – it had gone on like that for generation after generation, father giving place to son. Aunt visited this shop every day at some hour. Beyond the Chettiar shop was a shrine of Ganesha, which she visited every evening, and sat placidly with others in the corridor, listening to a pundit's narration of the epics.

All through the day Aunt lived in anticipation of the evening programme. The moment her day's duties were over, she locked up the front door and disappeared. If Raman returned home earlier, he stopped by the temple gate and tried to catch her attention. Invariably, within ten minutes, Aunt would turn round and notice him; It's telepathy, every time, he told himself. Stepping over the shoulders and heads of the assembly she would hold out the key to him, whispering, 'Do you want me?'

'No. Go back to your story.'

'In the almirah, I've kept –' she would mention some food or drink. As he retreated from the portals of the temple, with the key, he would reflect, She thinks I starve all day, fears I shall fall down in a faint unless she nourishes – food is her fixation. The voice from the temple would now float on the air: 'And when God came down . . .' Always bringing down God. On such easy terms with the Almighty!

What an awful lonely home, he generally reflected, when entering his house, and before lighting up. It seemed particularly unwelcome at that hour, until he passed to the back yard where the river flowed softly and birds on the trees over the steps created a din before settling down for the night. Men sat around in groups, some walked along the sands; women were filling their pitchers or washing clothes along the river's edge. Raman could watch it all over the wall. His back veranda, roofed with thatch, was his work-shed, where he kept his wooden planks, tools, and a kerosene lantern which he lit when working at night.

Must design and finish that piece of work for the Family Planning, Raman told himself one evening. He took down a plank from the wall, ran his fingers over it. Too smooth, the base white will run off, he reflected. Plane it a little rough. He took out the little plane, ran it over, and ran his finger along and felt its surface. He took out a can of paint, dipped the brush in, laid a couple of strokes along the plank's surface, and put it away to dry, leaning it against the wall with the painted side towards the wall. Don't want more stucco effect, enough trouble with that lawyer. He took from his pocket a piece of paper and studied the message on it. He didn't wish to risk a mistake and then have endless correspondence and arguments at the time of the settlement of bills. He studied the message closely. 'Family Planning Centre. Free Advice.' Population! Population! What a worry! Why not offer a bonus for those who remain single – like himself? No marriage means no children – no, not necessarily no children! The town hall veranda and the pavements around the market, the no-man's lands of Malgudi, swarmed with children of all sizes, from toddlers to four-footers, dust-covered, ragged – a visible development in five years. At this rate, they would overrun the globe – no harm; though they looked famished, their brown or dark skin shone with health and their liquid eyes sparkled with life. Where did they come from? Who noticed the wedding ceremonies of their parents? Or who were their parents? Perhaps there was nothing wrong in their coming into the world. They had as much right to be here as anyone else, more mouths to feed – all right, find more stuff for the mouths, that's all. One thing leads to another. Raman's thoughts went on to the production of food, lands lying fallow, and so forth. He told himself: I am not doing the right thing in carrying on with this sign-board painting. I took it up because I loved calligraphy; loved letters, their shape and stance and shade. But no one cares for it, no one notices these values. Like that bangle-seller and the lawyer and the other, who demand their own style and won't pay otherwise. Compromise, compromise; and now this family planner wants – God knows what – black and white, or white and black, shaded or plain? A job anyone could do, even that hack who works for Jayaraj.

But the job had come to him. They might order more if this turned out all right.

His thoughts hovered around the person who had commissioned this work. She called herself just Daisy. She was a slender girl in a sari. No one could say who was her husband or father or brother, or where she came from – a sudden descent on Malgudi. Daisy! What a name for someone who looked so very Indian, traditional, and gentle! One would expect a person on this job to be somewhat matronly, like the Mother Superior in the convent – large, broad-faced, towering over others, an executive type who could with a flourish of her arms order people about. But this girl looked like a minor dancer. He felt he ought to know more about her. He could not observe her too closely at their first meeting in her office situated in the New Block on Market Road. While she sat behind her desk, he had had no means of judging her nether half; he kept thinking that perhaps if she got up she would look tall and broad-based.

The town's busybody, Veerappa, owned the New Block and rented it out to offices. He had been Raman's friend in their college days and occasionally met him at The Boardless; now he was responsible for introducing him to Daisy of the Family Planning Centre. But he had proved obtrusive and talkative during the meeting, would not give a moment's respite for Raman to study the woman properly. Raman had liked Daisy's voice, thought it was a little masculine, and he would have preferred to listen to it without interruption, but Veerappa thrust himself forward and chattered continuously. Raman would have liked to sit looking at her, to judge her build and personality, but this man constantly nudged him and distracted his attention with his, 'Look, see here,' and 'You know what,' etc. . . . Raman had invented problems in order to be able to ply her with questions; but it was this chap who butted in and answered them.

'What's the over-all length?' Raman asked, but before he could complete his question, Veerappa answered, 'That you know best. I'm sure the lady is going to leave it to you.'

Raman wanted to stop to ask, Why is she calling herself Daisy? Daisy What? But he lacked the courage. He was sure if the question were put, Veerappa would give some answer promptly. Who was her protector, and what happened to him, that this slender creature should be left to tackle the population problems of this nation single-handed?' Was her complexion dusky or fair, eyes round or touched up? What shape of nose did she have? These were some of the important points that Raman wished to clear up. He felt that sign-board painting was after all proving worth while. It was an important link in society, among various types of people and their activities. But for sign-boards, people would wallow in isolation, no one would know what another was doing or what was happening.

He wished he could question her about herself, discreetly, inter-spersed with technical points relating to the sign-board. Luckily, when Veerappa left them for a moment in order to blow his nose and inhale a pinch of snuff, Raman managed to squeeze in a question as to where she lived.

'Not far from here, an outhouse in the Third Cross, Number Seven, to be entered by the side gate opening on the Fourth Cross, so that one need not go through the main gate.' When Veerappa came back giving some explanation as to why he had gone out, Raman looked satisfied, as if he had arrived at a secret understanding with Daisy, who, he imagined, looked significantly in his direction as if to confirm their sudden intimacy.

That had happened a couple of hours ago. Now he wished he could go back to her and clear one or two doubts occurring to him suddenly. But having been in her office all evening, it might look odd to go after her again. He was not sure if she would open the door for him – or whether she might choose to clear his doubts through the window-bars. He was now determined to give her the best possible service and please her; he lovingly selected the planks for her; he'd get the new sepia paint, which would give the work a touch of class. He felt again a surging impulse to cycle up and visit her, but held himself back. Must not make a fool of myself, he thought, a fellow whose outlook is to place sex in its place. To pursue a female after seeing only the upper half, above the desk – she might be one-legged, after all. But this is not sex which is driving me, but a normal curiosity about another person, that's all.

Next evening, after arriving at Number Seven by the side gate on Fourth Cross, he spent a long moment with his nose close to the door, unable to decide whether to knock or turn round and leave quietly. If the door suddenly opened and he were to be seen receding down the steps, she might consider him a crook, or if, while he hesitated, the door opened without his knocking, he might find himself face to face, within an inch of her, and that would be even more awkward. He decided to knock, and the knocking had to be not with his palms as if battering the door, like a boor, but with the knuckles of his right forefinger, properly crooked, a couple of taps, a pause, and tap, and if no response, he should retreat softly in a dignified manner. A soft knock, a gentle knock could convey the quality of the visitor; it should be like a musical note (as much as could be extracted from a wooden panel), conveying noble intentions. His mind sizzling with these plans and possibilities he knocked on the door, with measured distance between his finger and the door, as if executing some precision task. He heard a stirring on the other side of the door. Suppose she had a lover, and had to disengage herself suddenly? While this speculation troubled his mind, the voice inside asked, 'Who is there?'

Would she know if he mentioned his name? Could he say, 'Signboard painter'? For the first time he realized the unimpressiveness of his designation and wished he could all himself a 'lettering artist' – but even that sounded absurd and roundabout.

'I'm Raman, we met last evening, I came to your office.'

The door opened, and there she stood like a vision. He felt confused and once again found himself unable to assess her personality, saw her as in a mist. 'Oh! It's you!' she said. 'Come in.' He crossed the threshold hesitantly, wondering how to explain his business – actually no business. There seemed to be no one else in her house – courageous of her to admit a fellow in. He left the door open, unable to decide what he should do about it. He was going through a series of moments of indecision. Never had he been in such a predicament. He wished he had not embarked on this adventure. She said, 'Come in, come in,' and he felt like explaining, I was afraid . . . people might mistake us . . . He hoped his personality was showing up favourably. There was a single folding chair in a corner, and she moved it up and gestured him to sit down. He hesitated and said, 'Don't trouble yourself. I can be standing. Please sit down yourself.' She turned round, went into an inner room and returned carrying a stool, placed it against the wall, and sat down leaning on the wall. She indicated the chair again, and there ensued a pause, as if she waited for his opening sentence to inaugurate the meeting.

'I was passing this way, and you remember you were good enough to tell me where you lived.'

'You had asked for it,' she said coldly.

'Yes, yes. I wanted to know because –' and she watched intently for him to complete the sentence. He had nothing to complete it with, and only added, 'I was passing this way . . .'

'Where?' she asked.

'Eh . . . eh . . . to meet a friend in Kabir Street. A lawyer,' he added, without waiting for her to cross-examine, mentioning the first name that came to his head. 'He owes me money. That apart I wanted to see you. Would you like the letters on the sign-board to slant a bit and shaded with sepia tint?'

'I don't know,' she said. Her tone was both firm and gentle. She seemed to know her mind and its limits. The conversation seemed to collapse. Raman never imagined it would conclude so abruptly. He had prepared himself for this visit with the utmost care. Kept awake half the night thinking of it; roused himself from dreams relevant and irrelevant to his mood, and dressed himself with care – a light yellow bush-coat and white trousers with the creases in perfect shape; shaved his chin to a gloss; combed his hair back, applying brilliantine.

His aunt had been constrained to question his sudden interest in grooming himself so thoroughly. He dismissed her questioning indifferently, and said, 'Don't expect me to explain everything I do, and all the time.' She accepted the snub cheerfully, as she always did. This was an established mode of contact between them. Raman proved extremely considerate to her at times and extremely rude at other times, but the lady accepted with equal composure both treatments. She brought him a dish of some delicacy to his room. While he ate, she explained, 'This is something they don't do in this part of the country; it's known only in Poona.' He knew she would revert to her grandfather's Poona days. He had heard the story piecemeal again and again – how her grandfather had run away after his marriage, deserting his young wife, how years later his grandmother went after him, walking all the way with pilgrims going north, and had cornered her husband while he was living with his concubine in Poona, in grand style. He had heard this story often enough, but had to hear it again and again out of consideration for her. Some days, when his mind was preoccupied, he just got up and left in the middle of the narrative. But when his mood was tranquil and receptive, he listened to it again and again – how grandmother managed to get her husband to trek back southward, how he had brought his concubine along also but only up to Bangalore, midway in their journey, where the grandmother rushed neck deep into a lake and threatened to drown unless the concubine was abandoned, whereupon the grandfather somehow rid himself of the woman, and proceeded onward and settled down in his original home at Kumbakonam to a happy life. The good lady bore him several sons and daughters and died when her husband was seventy-five years old; thereafter he married again (just to spite his eldest son, who had slighted him in some way), a girl of seventeen, whose parents were after his wealth and ultimately poisoned him. That was the end of the Poona grandee. Raman's aunt remembered being carried in the arms of her mother during his funeral.

Now, sitting in Daisy's parlour, he was desperately trying to continue the conversation. She had slipped through a curtained door and brought him a cup of tea and salt biscuits. He noticed her figure and was satisfied with her proportions; not too tall – just tall enough to suit his height. He wondered why he should measure her against him. Not his business. Nothing to do with him. He looked about. The walls were bare, no furniture of any kind, and bundles of paper in a corner and dust-covered magazines. It was the hour between evening and night with no lights on yet. He liked this half-lit hour – it suited his pensive mood. It suited her complexion, he thought, which was a translucent brown – the best complexion that the human skin could attain. He drank the tea with many murmurs of appreciation. He asked, 'What about you?' She muttered some excuse. He found her reserved and not very communicative. No chance to seek any clarification about her antecedents. One could only hope that if she were married, her husband had deserted her. He was aware that it was he that was doing much of the talking. He explained his philosophy of letters grandiosely: 'You see, madam –' he realized that he was not even told her full name. He resented it, as if it were his right to be told everything. He was several times on the point of stopping to demand, What exactly is your real name, by which persons close to you know you? but he checked himself. There was a firmness, a calculated coldness in her look, which came through her elegance and femininity and discouraged one from taking chances with her. So he went on elaborating his philosophy of letters. 'You see, madam, whatever the language, the letters must have backbone and stand up to deliver the message, in unmistakable terms. I hate supine letters that bend low and crawl and cringe for attention and are floral. There was, for instance, a bangle-seller who wanted to be strict in cash matters, but afraid to say so – I refused to rewrite his sign to his order; you would have had to hide the word "cash" obscurely and let your customers search for it with a lens, surely!' This idea seemed to amuse her, and there was just a trace of a smile in that beautiful face. Encouraged by it, Raman repeated, 'I refused to rewrite and took away the plank, though it meant a waste of several days' work and a special plank of wood.' He felt heroic, and slightly drew himself up.

There was some sign of thawing, as she asked, 'Do you think you could be so assertive and firm in conveying a message for population control?' He paused to consider how best to answer without upsetting this divine creature. If it had been his circle at The Boardless restaurant, he would have slyly played about with the words 'population' and 'copulation'. A person who dealt in this kind of propaganda should not be squeamish, or pretend that population grew by itself. He studied her face for a moment to detect, if possible, some encouragement. But she looked business-like and detached, like a zoologist watching an ant. He said quietly, 'Yes, of course.'

He realized that it was time to leave. She was looking at the calendar on the wall and the timepiece. 'I hope I am not keeping you waiting?'

'For what?' she asked.

He wondered what she meant, and said, 'Maybe you have something to do.'

'Some women will be coming to see me.'

What sort of women? he wanted to ask, but forbore. They'd probably talk all evening on how to avoid pregnancy.

On his way home, he realized that he had not really discussed the sign-board or the business aspect. She had dismissed the whole issue in one sentence: 'I don't know,' and had only specified later that a proper red triangle must be painted at one corner of the board, since it happened to be the symbol of Family Planning, and was found on letter-heads, sign-boards, and everything connected with it. He wanted to utter a caution that the red triangle was likely to defeat their purpose, by acting as a sort of physical reminder rousing the baser instincts in some men. But that was none of his business. Anyway, a great responsibility was on him now, and he would show her his design at some stage and rectify any errors, since he would not like to engage himself in any sort of controversy with her later.

He'd probably carry the half-finished plank and show it to her for approval – but that would be unpractical. People who saw it on the road might smile and joke. If that wag and rival Jayaraj ever set eyes on it, that would be the end. He might build upon it a frightful edifice of scandal and make it difficult for Daisy to survive here. On the way home, he stopped by at the temple to take the key from his aunt. She got up from the assembly and handed him the key with the usual advice about food. It was eight o'clock and the story-telling would go on for at least a couple of hours more. 'Today, he is going to narrate Krishna's wedding with Rukmini, and I want to stay through.'

'Certainly. Don't hurry back. I'll look after myself.'

He put away his bicycle on the veranda of his house, but did not open the door. He went past his house, turned to his left on the rough track, ploughed through the sands, and sat on the top of the river-steps. With the stars above, and the faintly gleaming water flowing downriver with a soft splash, he felt a strange equanimity, and fell into a fit of introspection. All through the evening, he had behaved like a fool, had spoken words without any relevance. Tried to . . . tried to do what? Present himself as an all-important man. This visit itself was ill-motivated. Tried to invent problems and miserably failed. Succeeded in being incoherent, that was all. I'm sex-obsessed, that's all, to admit the plain fact. The first exposure to a sari-clad figure, and I drop everything and run after it. What excuse could I have for knocking on the door of a woman living by herself? She was quite generous in letting him in. She could have easily shut the door in his face. He brooded for a minute on the significance of her letting him in – was it possible that she cared for him? He tried to go over all her words of the evening. Not one sentence could be interpreted romantically. Remembrance of his own words filled him with shame and disgust. He had defeated his own image and cheapened it. Her words were brief, to the point, and with the occasional 'why' or a 'what' from her he became muddled and never gave a proper answer.

Our puranas were full of instances of saints failing in the presence of beauty. The gods grew jealous of austere men and manoeuvred to disturb their rigours, and their purpose; their agency was always a woman of beauty. Now the same situation was presenting itself in the garb of a Daisy. He had determined to give sex its place, and somehow the gods didn't seem to like it. Having written sign-boards for so many years, it was rather strange that he should be presented with a female customer now, and that it should prove so troublesome. He was going to shield himself against this temptation. Mahatma Gandhi had advised one of his followers in a similar situation, 'Walk with your eyes fixed on your toes during the day, and on the stars at night.' He was going to do the same thing with this woman. He would not look at her eyes when he met her, nor involve himself in any conversation beyond the strictest business. That business part of it was most important. To deliver the board next week, and take more orders if it was satisfactory.

He carried the half-finished plank, tied to his cycle-bar, and met her at her office at the New Block. She had a couple of visitors with her. They were all talking in a low tone, and their talk ceased when Raman entered the room. He stood at the door, paused for a moment, and said, 'I can come later, if you please.'

'Yes,' said the lady drily, and noticing the board he was carrying, 'Is that our board?'

'Yes, it's only a trial writing, not final.'

'Leave it there and come back' – she glanced at her watch – 'in thirty minutes.'

'I'll come and unwrap it myself, the paint is still wet,' he said, leaning the board against the wall. He turned round and went out, shutting the door behind him. He was visiting her after six days, and she had not displayed surprise, interest, or any sort of emotion in meeting him now. Just as well. He would be saved if she did not flash her eyes on him, and he would follow Mahatma Gandhi's formula and look at the ground while talking. The eye was really the source of mischief. One's thoughts followed what the eye saw. Thoughts developed from sight. He would wear coloured glasses so that she might not note where he was looking.

He lounged about the Market Road. An arcade of some interesting little shops had developed in an abandoned alley down the road, displaying all kinds of trinkets, flashlights, cuff-links, and so forth, most of them being tacitly approved smugglers' outlets for forbidden goods unloaded on deserted coasts. Would it not be nice to write a sign-board to declare: SMUGGLERS' ARCADE – STRICTLY IMPORTED GOODS. He could design an interesting board for it, in a slightly blue background with a suggestion of the sea. But the traders here were strangers constantly disappearing and reappearing under new names, hence no sign-board would be feasible. A sign-board pinned things down to a sort of permanency – it gave things an air of being established. That was why he appreciated Daisy's efforts now. That meant she intended to be permanent. At the thought of her, he was conscious of a sudden racing of his pulse. Quiet, he told himself. Time to turn round. He saw what he had come looking for – sunglasses, a stall full of them. He picked up a pair and tried it; through the dark smoked glass he could hardly decipher the face of the shopman, who looked grotesque with his thick lips, square nose, and no chin. Very satisfactory. 'What's the price?'

'Fifty rupees . . .'

'Nonsense, I'll take it for ten.'

'It's from Hong Kong – make it fifteen . . .'

'Twelve,' and the bargain was over.

Two idlers watched this transaction with interest and one of them murmured. 'It's a good purchase . . .' Raman put on the glasses and looked at them. Their faces, too, looked monkeyish. He took off the glasses, found them not so monkeyish. Very satisfactory. He had come in a deliberate négligé today – a dhoti and a striped bush-coat – and if she spurned him for it, so much the better.

In exactly thirty minutes he was back in her office. As he was going up, Daisy's visitors were descending. He wore the dark glasses when he entered her room, hoping that she would think, This hideous fellow is back! She was waiting for him. He said very little, briskly removed the cover of the board, and held it up for her to see. She came very near – perfume, reminiscent of some strange herbs, wafted from her.

'Good,' she said, 'the letters are big enough to be seen from the street.'

'From fifty feet; this size lettering is meant for it, though it's somewhat more expensive per letter – more paint and more time are consumed . . .'

She stepped back and viewed the board. 'It seems all right to me, very clean work, I must say . . .'

'This is only a proof. When it is finished, it'll look perfect.'

'Perfect?' she repeated, raising her brow. Till now he had been talking to her with his eyes looking away, but now he lifted his eyes in her direction, looked through his glasses. He noticed that she seemed heavy-jowled and somewhat ridiculous, with her forehead slightly tapering. The Hong King optician has excelled in his art, he thought. She looks terrible. This is even better than Gandhi's plan to keep one's mind pure. She seemed to grin, and looked like a demoness! Soorpanaka's approach should have had the same effect on Rama, he reflected, recollecting an episode from the Ramayana. Her teeth seemed to jut out and were uneven. He smiled to himself. She was saying through her ridiculous mouth, 'Is there anything more you wish to do with it or will you finish it as it is?'

'It is up to you to tell me. I could perhaps give a red outline – a rectangular border, which will set off this red-triangle emblem at the corner. Does the ensign seem to you all right?'

She studied it closely, placing herself near and far. Each time she moved by his side a whiff of perfume hit his senses and made his resolution reel.

'If you like, I can shade the angles of all the vowels with sepia – they'll look decorative.'

'Go ahead, if you think so. I will trust you to do your work in the best manner possible. How long will you take to finish it?'

'Next week this day; if the weather continues sunny like this, it should be dry completely.' She didn't seem to notice his dhoti and the striped bush-shirt. 'Shall I pack it up?' he asked, and she nodded. He wrapped the paper around, tied it up, and made ready to leave.

'Are you in a hurry to go?' she asked suddenly.

He hesitated for half a second. If he had said 'Yes,' it might have made a lot of difference to his days ahead. But he hesitated between yes and no, and she decided it for him. 'Come and sit down for a while,' and he followed her sheepishly. She went back to her seat at the desk, and watched him in silence for a while. She asked suddenly, 'Why those glasses? Don't you find them a nuisance inside a room at this hour?'

He had to find an explanation. 'Some dust blew into my eyes –' he began to spin a yarn.

'Does it bother?' she asked.

'Slightly,' he said, without looking at her.

She suddenly came over and pulled off the glasses, and stared into his eyes. This action was so sudden that Raman could hardly comprehend what had been happening until she was back in her seat and said, 'I see nothing now. Perhaps you'll do well to give your eyes a wash. I have had some doctor's training, too, you know?'

'Oh, how wonderful!' he said, 'I'll come to you if I am in difficulty.'

She had not returned his glasses to him, but carried them with her, held them up against the light, waved them up and down and said, 'Throw this thing away, the lenses are uneven and full of errors. You'll become squint-eyed . . .'

'It's from Hong Kong,' he said by way of defence.

'No wonder,' she said, and he did not know what she meant.

He lay tossing in bed that night. She had touched him, and that had sent his blood-pressure up so high that he had felt giddy, and her perfume had nearly stunned him. He had stolen a glance at her when she was fumbling with the glasses on his nose. But she stood so close that he could not see her clearly; still, many points about her personality were puzzling. He told himself, I must get over this obsession. Till yesterday I was a free man with my mind unfettered. Today I am unable to think of any other subject. She has even deprived me of the glasses which would have helped my mental calm. He lay tossing all night. All kinds of dreams bothered him, every act was mixed up with that woman, She said several times, 'Come, dear, to my side,' and had no clothes on. When he woke up, he felt ashamed of himself. An edifice of self-discipline laboriously raised in a lifetime seemed to be crumbling down. He had chosen to remain a bachelor, in spite of the several opportunities that came his way to choose a bride for himself, if not at least to flirt with. That accountant-general from Nagpur and his daughter – what a beauty she was! – educated, urbane, tall, and flashy like a film star. How much they had tried to involve him in their set last year – the man had left his daughter unchaperoned with him in their room at Anand Bhavan Hotel, but he determinedly kept his distance from her and spurned the whole proposal for no other reason than that he would not be interested in women. He wished to establish that the man-woman relationship was not inevitable and that there were other more important things to do in life than marrying.

And then another and another. The girls who ogled him when he went to the college on business, and the parents of eligible girls sending down horoscopes, and all sorts of women who paused to look at him, as if ready to follow if beckoned. But he was resolute. He often told himself, The more they try, the more firmly will they be repulsed. He had steeled himself against this blunder committed by human beings since Adam. If Adam had possessed a firm mind, the entire course of creation would have taken a different turn. Mind conditioned by story-writers, poets, and dramatists from time immemorial who had no other theme than love – easiest subject to deal with. This philosophy had been my armour and made me unique all these years. Now am I on the verge of defeat?

Yes, said his truthful conscience. You are absolutely right. You are now in a different category. You are an honest man. Examine your thoughts, assay the contents of your deepest thoughts, see what there is. You are preoccupied with her physical form inch by inch all the time you are discussing the measurement of your sign-board. The clothes on her simply do not exist for you, you are preoccupied with what you can accidentally glimpse at, hoping for a chance to see her clothes blown off; while she sits away at her desk, you fancy her on your lap; while she is conversing, you are sealing her lips with your kiss. That is the tragedy of womanhood – utility articles whether in bed or out. You never view them normally until they are past sixty and look shrunken-skinned. Do you ever recollect the face of the woman whose thighs you so long meditated upon at the river-steps?

I am in bad shape, he told himself, sitting up in bed. I am a victim of some shock, and must get over it if I am not to make a fool of myself in this world. Finish her work completely and forget her, finish the transaction without raising my gaze to her.

In order to escape these thoughts, he switched on the light and picked up the *Planter's Story* and tried to read. The book was open, but his mind wandered and like an elastic returning to its starting point, back to Seven, Third Cross, facilely crossing the barriers of roads, distance, doors, and the darkness of the night. I wonder if she is also thinking of me! A flattering speculation.

His aunt asked from the other room, 'Aren't you asleep? Why still awake?'

He felt as usual irritated and that irritation was a momentary distraction from love-sickness. He put out the light in anger. I must explain everything, I suppose, to this old woman. I have no freedom. In darkness he confessed to himself. This is true love-sickness, I suppose. I used to laugh at this condition whenever I came across it in stories.

When the board was dry and ready, he carried it along, properly wrapped, to her office. With the board under his arm, he went up the staircase, resolutely saying to himself, No nonsense, strictly business. The eye leads the thoughts and the hand follows the mind and then outruns it.

'I thought I would never see you again!' she cried when he stood on the landing. 'What had you done with yourself?'

'I was busy,' he said briefly, doing his best not to look at her eyes. She probably hypnotizes, he thought; safer to look at her as little as possible. 'This is ready,' he said, and unwrapped the board and leaned it against the wall, like an artist showing his new painting.

She looked at it from a distance and then came nearer and saw it, nodded her head in approval. 'Good,' she said.

'Would you like to hang it up now?' he asked in what he believed to be a purely business-like tone.

She just said, 'Yes, I will show you the place. Come with me.' She walked onto the veranda, leaned over the balcony, and pointed to a spot on the roadside wall. He kept his look strictly where she was pointing, although he wanted to gaze on her in the sunlight and watch her curves straining through her sari as she bent over the parapet. She is a siren, planning to eat me up, I suppose. I must be careful, he thought. She was saying, 'It would be best to have it here, but how will you get up here?'

He moved up beside her with downcast eyes, and looked out. The Market Road traffic and pedestrians were interesting to watch from here – a colourful kaleidoscope. He was lost in this vision for a few seconds while Daisy watched him surreptitiously, as it seemed to him. He asked, 'Do you want this nailed up now?'

'Yes, should I get you some help?'

'No,' he said. 'Fixing up the board is a part of my job, I can do it. You don't have to wait for it; you may attend to your work while I finish it.' There was a wry smile on her face. He felt that he had spoken too much. He felt heroic as he vaulted over the parapet, stood on a ledge, and surveyed the spot. He took out a pencil and scale, marked the exact position, and asked, 'Is this all right?' She leaned over again and he could see the top of her head almost touching his and the perfume lulled his senses, almost defeating his resolutions. She has lovely natural waves, he commented to himself.

She said, 'It is all right, but I feel nervous while you stand there.'

He felt rather pleased at her concern, but overcame it. What is it to her if I fall off? What am I to her? These are the well-known tricks of wily women. Must not be taken in by it. He hopped back to the veranda, went across the room to fetch the board. He took out of his Gandhi-print bag nails and a hammer. When she asked, 'Shall I hold it?' he just shook his head; with the board in one hand, he jumped onto the ledge again, and in a few minutes had nailed it securely, and was back on the veranda with a flicker of a smile on his face.

He took out his kerchief and mopped his brow. 'Well, it is done,' he said to her. She leaned over once again to take a look at it and he half averted his eyes from her back bent over the wall. 'Is it all right?' he asked, and added, 'Perhaps you should inspect it from the road, if you can spare a moment to do it.'

She seemed pleased at the suggestion. Raman picked up his bag, ready to go down the staircase. He stood aside at the landing to let her pass. This should give me a chance to see her in sunlight, he reflected, and at once scotched the thought. He followed her down, striving his best not to watch her back, looking fixedly at his own feet. They came out of the building; already there were people standing on the pavement and reading the sign aloud, and commenting among themselves. The two crossed the street and stood on the other edge of the road. A side glance convinced him that the full sunlight on her face made no difference to her complexion, only he noticed a faint down on her upper lip and the vestige of a pimple on her right cheek. Her eyes seemed to acquire extra brilliance in the sunlight. That is an unnatural gleam, a sure sign that she is a siren, he thought, strengthening the self-protective forces within. Looking up, she said, 'Very clear and the letters shaded so well stand out.'

'That should bring in a lot of visitors and keep you busy,' he said, feeling that he should say something pleasant after all, because he was going to take leave of her. They walked back to the building; one or two acquaintances of Raman's nodded, smiled, and passed. The sign seemed somehow to make people smile. At the building Raman took his bicycle from its stand, and prepared to depart.

She said, 'Your bill?'

'I will send it by post, and you can send me a cheque.' he said and mumbled, 'Good-bye, thanks.'

'Thank you for your help,' she whispered with her foot on the staircase.

This will pass, truly, said Raman to himself. It has passed, I have escaped. No more reason to see her again. He cycled up and down, sought the company of his friends at The Boardless, with a feeling of relief that again he would be in the company of men who would not affect his own temper and temperament in all those strange ways, with whom he could speak thoughtlessly, irresponsibly, and even licentiously, and also make a few jokes about birth-control. The seriousness and solemnity that he had to maintain in the presence of the lady got on his nerves, and of course there were also the unfathomable psychological disturbances that she caused by her siren-like ways. Showing concern for him when he had his foot on the balcony, pretending to help and wanting to hold the board or the bag – always trying to reach out to him. He was not one who could be deceived by such tricks. She had hoped, perhaps, that their hands would touch. And all that straining over the wall with her bodice nearly bursting! That was most unseemly. He could see through all those tricks and, thank God, he had had enough self-control and indifference – otherwise that office room would have become a love-chamber in no time. He congratulated himself especially on the smart and clipped manner in which he had spoken about the bill coming by post, and he could see that she was shaken by his stern manner. Bicycling along, his mind was as usual very busy, now, at the task of analysing; there was a great deal of misreading and exaggeration while brooding over her actions and speech, but it was only a reaction from his previous state of complete surrender; and it gave him a feeling of being strong and uninfluenceable. When I need a wife, I will know how to set about it, all in good time. I don't have to succumb to the first female brushing against me, he said to himself, and continued the discussion on the same lines when he met his friends over coffee at The Boardless.

Part Two

It was an awkward moment. He was not prepared to receive any visitor, least of all the girl. He had been having a nap in the afternoon, falling asleep over a volume of verse. His aunt woke him up: 'Ram . . . Ram, get up. There is a girl at the door to see you. Who is she?'

'I don't know,' he said, befuddled with sleep. 'Speak to her, I won't get up now.' He turned over and slept again. He was aware of Aunt's standing there for a little while and then fading out. When he woke up again, he heard a voice in the kitchen. He got up and looked in. Daisy was seated on a mat outside the kitchen, sipping coffee. Oh, God! Here she is! Me to be seen in this state! His aunt's voice was coming from within the kitchen. She was reminiscing as usual. Daisy looked rather domesticated in these surroundings, sitting comfortably on a small mat, with her back to him. He was barebodied, wearing a dhoti. No need to take pains to make himself unpresentable now; if she saw him in his present state, she would have no illusions about him, and that would be the best antidote for love-sickness in case she suffered from it; better than distorting goggles. He tiptoed back silently, before his aunt should notice. Otherwise that garrulous creature would indiscreetly hail him. 'All the way, my grandfather walked back from Poona . . .' she was saying. That'd be a long narration, and Raman retreated quietly, wondering why Daisy should have come in search of him. After hanging up the sign-board at her office, he had kept away from her. He had sent the bill for the work. That was two weeks ago. After that he had resumed his normal activities – painting and reading and political analysis and gossip at The Boardless. He had expected his cheque to arrive by post, and avoided the Family Planning area. He had resolutely avoided any thought of her. He wanted to retain his sobriety. But here she was under his very roof. His mind was in a confusion. If I dress and slip away by the back door, he speculated, nothing terrible is going to happen. After all, she is here on her own. I didn't ask her. Aunt has received her and can dispose of her; she can have her fill of reminiscences.

In a half hour, he washed, groomed, and made himself fit to be seen by a queen. Still with her back to him, sitting at the kitchen entrance, Daisy was engrossed in Aunt's narrative. Must by this time be familiar with all that happened on the highway, and the concubine's exit. Raman cried with extra gusto, 'Ah! what an unexpected pleasure and privilege. Sorry I was asleep.'

Daisy turned round and said, 'Your aunt has kept me engaged. I didn't notice the time passing.'

Aunt came out of the kitchen saying, 'She has told me all about her duties. Isn't it by God's will that children are born?'

'But our government does not agree with God,' Raman said. Daisy got up, ignoring the joke. Raman said breezily, 'I am sorry, I don't have chairs; we manage with mats.'

She said, 'Oh, what does it matter, where we sit? It's all the same to me. I did not see a chair till I was eighteen. In our village no chair was to be seen except one in the village munsif's house; even that was brought out only when the collector came on an inspection.'

Aunt said, 'Chairs are bad for the limbs and joints, people lose their flexibility. Sitting on the floor and rising is the best way to keep from growing fat.'

'Those who grow fat will do so, whether they sit down on the floor or chair . . . it's not that,' said Daisy, contradicting Aunt. All of a sudden, Raman put an end to this discussion with, 'I'm comfortable here and won't exchange it for a palace.'

Daisy now came up, took out of her handbag an envelope. 'I thought I might fetch your cheque in person, I had the address on your letter, you know . . .'

Raman received the envelope with murmurs of thanks, led her to his room, and seated her on the mat. He said apologetically, 'I let my aunt run this house in her own way and see no need to interfere. This is our old ancestral house, you see.'

She said, 'How lucky to have a river running in your back yard! I noticed it the first thing when I came in.' After some further palaver, Daisy said, 'I have now come to ask if you are prepared to do a little work outside in some of the villages. We have an intensive campaign in rural areas.'

'What would you expect me to do?'

'I am going on a tour of the surrounding villages for an initial survey, and to look out for places where we can write our message on the walls permanently. The headquarters want a picture of a family

– a couple with two children, with the message "We are two; let ours be two; limit your family" – in all the local languages.'

Raman could not share her seriousness and began to laugh.

She was offended and said, 'I see no joke in this.'

He had to explain away his levity. 'No, no, not connected with this. I was thinking of something my aunt was saying.'

'About what?' Daisy asked relentlessly. She had grown slightly red in the face. It seemed as if her faith had been abused. Such missionary zeal! 'Don't you see how horrible it is with everything crowded, and an endless chain of queues for food, shelter, bus, medicine, and everything, with thousands of children coming with nothing to eat, no clothes to wear, no roof, no civilized existence being possible on such a mass scale – each one of us has to do our bit in the corner of the country allotted to us.' He had not suspected that she would feel so strongly on this subject. As far as he was concerned, it was purely professional – his duty being to inscribe whatever he was ordered – and he could not share anyone's passion for the cause. But he still had to take care not to offend this fair creature seated before him and demanding his faith. She lapsed into silence and he felt he had to say something to cheer her up. He assumed a grave look and said, 'Of course, it's all very sad and thoughtless . . .'

'What?' she questioned abruptly.

He was at a loss to explain, nervous lest he should upset her again by saying the wrong things. He said in a general way, 'I mean, it's a national tragedy – looked at from the right perspective.' She looked appeased, and continued to expatiate on her plans. He realized that she was a zealot on the population question and that he should not trifle with her feelings. All the world's workers who had any results to show were fanatics, he reminded himself. If she were a despotic queen of ancient days, she would have ordered the sawing off of the organs of generation. He realized he had been mistaken in taking her to be just a suave bureaucrat who got sign-boards written and files completed and properly knotted with red tape while within she seemed to carry a furnace of conviction.

Raman was subject to further revelations in the next three weeks they spent together travelling and campaigning in the countryside. He lost count of days, distances, directions, of the names of the places visited. Daisy had a steel-framed itinerary and followed it scrupulously. They travelled by taxi, bus, train, and even lorry. Daisy's only aim was to reach a particular village and complete her work there. Her adaptability was astonishing; she could spread out the little roll of carpet that she carried in a bag and sleep anywhere. She also carried a little food container and a bottle of drinking water, and had suggested to Raman to equip himself similarly. Wherever she could, she filled up the containers with what was available – egg, bread, chicken, meat, fruit, or rice. She had no taboo of any kind. Raman, though brought up as a strict vegetarian, tried to eat for her sake and suffered in silence. It made him sick – it seemed impossible to bite into fish; when he ate meat, he had the feeling of burrowing into the side of some quadruped. They ate in the veranda of a rest-house or a village schoolroom or in the mottled shade of a coconut grove. She bathed in a public well, washed and dried her clothes after ordering Raman to keep away. She never bothered about comforts, conveniences. She accepted any hospitality, even in the lowliest hut, and proved extremely undemanding.

She explained, 'Let us live at least for a while as millions of our population live; otherwise we will never understand our own people. Living in a city is not the real life. Urban life is standardized, and meant to keep people apart.'

'Then why do you live in the city?'

'Ultimately I'll select the tiniest hamlet and live in a hut. I'll not want anything more than what a majority of our population have.'

'Are you a communist?' Raman asked suddenly.

She glared at him. 'What if I am or if I am not? Is there a label one should always carry like a dog-collar? . . .' They had had their lunch in the classroom of a children's school, and were resting for half an hour, as she always insisted. At unexpected moments, she became intense and red in the face, leaving Raman wondering how he could have upset her. He did not pursue the inquiry. Any question he might ask seemed to upset her. He remained quiet as a safety-first measure. She herself added, 'I like to serve the people in what seems to me the best way, that's all. And in this area allotted to me now, if I can help arrest the population growth by even five per cent within this year, I'll be satisfied.' Raman felt bewildered by her intensity. Wanted to ask, Why such anger? Why not accomplish it all with less grimness?

He made a series of discoveries about her from time to time. She had a smiling side to her and a non-smiling one; a talkative and non-speaking. She smiled when she could forget her mission, and became grim when the population problems oppressed her mind. He never suspected that anyone could be personally so affected by population. After all, he often reflected, she should be satisfied if I write the boards clearly, and not expect me to go through it as a religious exercise. Often he was on the point of cracking a joke, but controlled himself. He realized that he was becoming extremely considerate of her feelings – not as if he were dealing with a woman purely on a business footing – it seemed more like a considerate husband and an irritable wife.

Why will she not be my wife? Time enough, time enough, he told himself. She may throw me out if I speak of it now. I can't say she is the gentlest person I have known. She looks frail, but not gentle. In any case when she becomes a wife and proves tough and argument- ative and red in the face, repulses my companions at The Boardless and that bookseller, and flings out my rare editions . . . I don't know. Thoughts floated across his mind like wisps of cloud across the sky – coming on from somewhere and vanishing as he sat beside her in a bus and watched the trees and landscape glide by . . .

At every place, she had the same routine. She had a perfect time- table between her arrival and departure. Settled down at the local school or on the veranda of a hospitable home or hut or in the shade of a tree. Sent Raman out to select a wall for their inscription, met the local official or the village headman and with his help collected data and statistics, called for the register of births and deaths, and took notes in her diary. Summoned an audience of men, women, and children under the big tree, and spoke to them quietly, firmly, with conviction. Explained to them the process of birth and its control. Daisy explained physiology, anatomy, and sexual intercourse, with charts or, if a blackboard was available, with sketches in chalk. She never felt shy or hesitant, but sounded casual. Sometimes the men sniggered, the women giggled, but she quietened them with a word or gesture. Sometimes the elders tried to send away the children. But she commanded, 'Let them also stay. It's important for them, more than for their elders,' and kept them around, although she was not really a lover of children and viewed them perhaps as symbols of defeat for her cause. She never patted a child or tried any baby talk. She looked at them as if to say, You had no business to arrive – you lengthen the queues, that's all.

When Raman had selected a wide side-wall of a house or temple, she viewed it from various angles and distances, negotiated for its lease with the owner, and gave Raman instructions. 'We shall only select the spots now. Later on you will come back and write the signs. In all about thirty I am planning now. You will have to come round later and finish the work as quickly as possible. When the message has sunk into their minds, I'll come again with a medical team, who'll do vasectomies and also fit up contraceptive devices. I am preparing them for it in this visit. A great deal will depend upon how quickly you'll finish your work so that they'll get used to the idea. We'll give you an allowance to take an assistant with you, but paint and brush will have to be provided by you.'

He wanted to say, I hope you'll also be around. I shall feel the emptiness of the world when you are away, but he swallowed back his words and she asked, 'What are you trying to say?'

He just said, 'Some advance may be required for buying brush and paint.'

'Oh, yes, of course whatever you want.'

When he found her in a 'smiling mood', he tried to question her about her life. She was relaxed whenever they completed a task in a village and were ready to catch the bus or a country cart for the next village. She did not mind the long waits for a bus under a wayside tree or even in the sun. If she found an upturned packing case or a stone slab, she sat on it, cross-legged, and never stirred until the bus came, without saying a word or noticing the people who stared at her. In order to be unnoticeable, she wore a sari of the drabbest shade, never used any powder or make-up, and did her hair up indifferently, and if it was ruffled in the wind, she smoothed it out with her palm. Still, there was much charm about her, and the village people generally stood around to gaze at her. Sometimes they thought she was a doctor out to perform abortions. Instead of feeling outraged at the notion, she would explain her mission with patience. Once at a village, while they waited for a bus, a villager came and requested, 'Please come to my cottage.'

'I may miss the bus,' she replied. He was importunate. She said to Raman, 'Let us go and see.'

The villager looked forlorn, and led the way to a cottage not far from the bus-stand. At the door of the cottage, the men stayed back. He said, 'Doctor, please go in and speak to my woman.'

Daisy remained inside the hut for some time, conversing in a low voice, came out, and said to the villager, 'Ten childbirths in twelve years of married life: don't you see that it will kill your wife?'

'True. She is very sickly,' admitted the man. 'I have to spend so much on medicines for her, but nothing helps.'

'And the children?' she inquired.

'Six died,' he added sorrowfully. 'God gives and he takes away . . . and that's why I thought at least now . . .'

She turned to Raman and said with a sad smile, ' They think I can abort!'

At which Raman tried to explain to the villager what Daisy and he were there for, but the villager kept pleading, 'If only the doctor makes up her mind to help us . . .'

Daisy said firmly to him, 'At least, prevent the next child coming. Other doctors will be here next month. Let this baby come; can't be stopped now.' The villager escorted them back to the bus-stop, saying the same thing over and over again and pleading repeatedly all the way. Daisy became very silent and was sullen until they were in the bus, when she said, 'Poor fellow! Ninety per cent of our masses are at this level. We have an uphill task. But we shall do it. A five per cent improvement in a year will satisfy me.' She looked gratified at this possibility and sat brooding. It looked as though she feared if she weren't strict an entire crowd of newborns would be clamouring and howling at her door. But Raman restrained himself from saying so, and just asked, 'When did you get interested in this problem?'

She kept looking ahead at the passing scenery and said, 'Even when I was young. A missionary gentleman inspired me early in life.' She stopped short, not wishing to go over the past, a subject she always avoided.

They got off the bus at a cross-road leading on to the Mempi Hills. She said, 'No road, we are going on foot.' She hauled her baggage on to her back, and he did his likewise.

'How far do we have to walk?'

'Three miles, maybe four on a foot-track. We are going to a mountain village.'

Raman looked resigned to his fate. He had still four unfinished jobs waiting at his work-shed, past the delivery date. But how could he speak to her about it? She expected him to be as dedicated as she was. He had said more than once, 'For my part, I'll promise to write the messages as well as I can,' hinting that she should not expect more than that from him. She had taken it in her own way and had said, 'You serve in your own way, of course.' Raman thought, I have other customers and other signs to write. How can you expect me to be writing only DON'T MULTIPLY? You leave me no time for anything else. Her passion for service seemed to him carried too far. But he dared not comment.

He realized that he was gradually becoming overconsiderate. They probably mean this state when they say, 'Love is blind.' It probably also deadens the wits and makes one dumb. One likes to please the other at any cost. Otherwise how could I ever show this zest for birth-control? He brooded and introspected as he followed her mutely on the foot-tracks, criss-crossing the mountain-side. She climbed and moved with ease without a pause. Far below, the plains stretched away under the afternoon sun. She walked ahead wrapped in her own thoughts, not seeming to give a thought for him. She had offered him the privilege of accompanying her and he had accepted it, that was all. She treated him as a sort of a trailer. He felt a sudden irritation at this thought and wondered why he should not turn round and go back home; he glanced at his watch – four o'clock – the best hour at The Boardless, with fresh coffee percolating through the brass filter. As the evening advanced, they'd dilute it with hot water. Fragrant coffee was available only between three and four in the afternoon, the precise hour when his system craved it. But this woman seemed impervious to such needs – she was satisfied if she could eliminate pregnancies! That was food and drink for her. He was afraid to seek any information from her as to whether she had any arrangements for coffee at this time. She would spurn such a question and treat him as a infidel, thirsting for coffee when mother earth was groaning under the weight of excess population. He speculated on what would happen if he caught a couple of women in each village and went to bed with them and thus, in ten months, fouled up Daisy's anticipated five per cent improvement! Fantastic and morbid but, withal, a very entertaining day-dream. But such pursuits were beyond him, he was ignorant of the technique, also his general philosophy prevented such exercises. Or perhaps, he wondered, he lacked the normal virility. But if he were impotent, he would be just right for Daisy, who might feel her mission in life fulfilled by her husband. He realized that he was indulging in such wild, salacious thoughts because the woman was walking ahead without bothering to turn round to see if he was following. And then he explained to himself that, naturally, she had to walk ahead because she was the one who knew the way on that narrow path. Should. not indulge in bitter thoughts, he reminded himself. Her small knot of hair bobbing up and down as she swayed along somehow filled him with pity. He should run up and seize her and declare his love to her and beg her to leave the villagers alone and try to change the whole course of her life, or else become a true missionary himself for her sake. He wished he knew more about her, but she just snapped shut any reference to the past. What could be the mystery?

After panting up a never-ending slope, he was relieved to notice her pace slackening, as village homes came into view beyond a grove of mango and coconut trees. She stopped and waited for him to come up and said, breathing hard, 'Here we are after all . . . at least four miles from the main road.'

He felt happy, forgetting instantly all his annoyance. He noticed that her face had become red and covered with perspiration. He felt a pity for her travails. Why was she putting herself through these ordeals, when she could have married and relaxed at home, leaving it to a husband to sweat for her? People are moved by strange, inexplicable drives, he concluded. He asked, 'How did you know about this village?'

'Well, I study the map and the vital statistics before selecting the area of operations. I know my ground. Also, I have been here before,' she said. 'This is one place where concentrated work will be needed. The growth rate is frightening.'

A mild-looking man received them at the entrance to the village. 'He conducts the school here,' explained Daisy. Do you have such things as coffee? Raman wanted to inquire first.

The teacher led the way to his house and seated them on the *pyol* under a low, sloping tiled roof; a narrow doorway led to an inner court. The teacher's wife came out to welcome them, and invited Daisy to go in with her. The teacher explained, 'The lady came here last year and stayed with us a whole week . . . last year about this same time. This is the best time of the year. Next month when the monsoon breaks, we will be impounded for four months. It will be continuously raining.'

'How will you manage for buying food-stuff and so forth?'

'We stock most of our needs, as we also grow what we want . . . Anyway, when the downpour is not too heavy, we move about – sometimes the water comes as a deluge from the upper reaches, and then all hands will be turned to diverting the flood.' He went in and brought out a couple of bananas on a plate and a brass cup filled with purplish coffee. No kinship with the brew at The Boardless, Raman sighed, but he drank it and felt revived. 'You could stay with us,' the teacher said. ' The lady can sleep inside, and we will sleep on this *pyol*. I think you should rest after the walk.'

But Daisy did not seem to need rest. In a few moments, she emerged from the house with her hair brushed back, and joined them. She said, 'Our work must start right away, before the monsoon begins, as it has been observed that the birth-rate goes up during the monsoon months.' The implications were clear that during the rains the village folk, cooped up in their homes, had no better business than to procreate. This notion was timidly contested by the teacher. A sort of debate ensued between them. She settled down on the *pyol* for a good, prolonged argument on the subject. The teacher looked mild, with a thin line of hair on his upper lip, but he had a lot of guts – as it seemed to Raman – to engage himself in a controversy with Daisy. She asked with a rather mischievous look, 'Well, can you explain exactly how people engage themselves when it's pouring all hours of the day for months?' She opened her handbag and took out her memo-book, made a note on some page, and waited for the man's answer.

The teacher said, 'When it rains, the main hall of the temple is filled with people. A pundit comes in that season and reads the Ramayana for forty days, a full course, from the birth of Rama to his coronation – it takes forty days and then the Mahabharata takes longer; by the time it is concluded, we reach the end of the season. We give the pundit a room in the temple and look after him.'

'Very well,' argued Daisy. 'At the end of the discourse-men and women do go home, don't they?' To Raman it seemed that she was obsessed with the sexual activities of others. Probably she did not have a clean mind. She had a pornographer's philosophy of life, perhaps. Otherwise why did her thoughts travel behind closed doors and revel in pictures of what people did when it was cold and damp outside?

The teacher said, 'And then that is the season when they clean up and store their grains, and attend to various things they could not do when they had to be out all day in other seasons. Please don't judge us harshly. I keep my school open, and they also assemble on this *pyol* without time-limit. Of course, I agree that some control of population is necessary, but I feel its evil is exaggerated.'

Daisy looked horrified on hearing it and declared, 'What is the population of this village now?'

'Seven hundred-odd,' said the teacher promptly.

Daisy said, 'It was just six hundred last year this time . . . and there is an increase of nearly twenty per cent. Has your food production increased twenty per cent? Have your accommodations increased twenty per cent? I know they haven't. Your production has increased only three per cent in spite of various improved methods of cultivation. Have more houses been built between the last monsoon and now? I know that the number of houses has remained the same for decades . . .' The teacher looked crest-fallen; which was a sort of admission of her thesis. He felt relieved that she was not questioning him on the size of his family; but presently, when several boys and girls of assorted sizes kept dashing in and out of his house and he found Daisy eyeing them questioningly, he volunteered the explanation: 'You see, they are children from the neighbouring houses, they have come to play with my children. I have only four . . .'

'I know, I know,' she said and added, 'You had only three when I was here last!'

What a lot of policing she was doing! Raman thought. She must really be mad! She will fight and shun people who bring up large families. Some madness must have got into her head quite early in life and stayed on there.

She explained to the teacher, 'Our quantum of population-increase every year is equal to the total population of a country like Peru, that's fourteen million.'

'What if!' said the foolhardy teacher. 'We have enough space in this country – still so many undeveloped areas.'

She was very patient with this dialectician. She said quietly, 'How many of the seven hundred-odd in this village will be prepared to move over to new areas when their homes become too congested?'

Raman felt like asking, How is it your concern? If people like to live crowded, it's their business. What a frightful bully you are turning out to be. Thank God, you are not a dictator.

The teacher explained, 'The families here are all stonemasons. They quarry stones and send them all over the country. Their business is to blast the mountain-side and cut and shape the stones.

At the moment, they have an order to cut and dress three thousand tons of slabs and blocks for a temple in America. It's quite a thriving business. Why will they move? They have to be where the mountain is. They cannot afford to leave its side.'

She said, 'Exactly. I am not suggesting that they uproot themselves, but if they want to stay comfortable, let them avoid creating an unmanageable crowd around themselves, that's all. I am not prohibiting anything, but only suggesting that they avoid too many children.'

She spoke on the same lines to the gathering which the teacher was able to muster under the banyan tree in the centre of the village. This had to be late in the evening next day, as she had to wait for the men and women to return from work, wash, and eat before coming out to listen to her. They had hung up a few lanterns from the branches of the tree. Men, women, and children squatted on the ground under the platform and eagerly looked up as if they were going to hear a Ramayana discourse. Helped by the teacher's explanations, she spoke to them for nearly an hour, and concluded by hoping that their village would have no more than seven hundred at the same time next year. Some elders of the village asked, 'God gives us children. How can we reject His gift?' She did not contradict the thesis outright, but gently presented a scientific, rational point of view. But when the chiefman said, 'There is an old shrine in a cave over there where barren women can go and pray and bear children. How would you explain it?' Daisy simply answered, 'You should ask the priest of that temple,' and Raman admired the courage and subtlety of her reply.

While others seemed to have taken this remark rather casually, or perhaps they were too innocent to follow its meaning, later, next day, the priest of the temple accosted them and challenged her comments. The shrine was a mile outside the village as one went down the slopes on the northern side. Raman had already gone round in search of a surface for writing. The blank outer wall of this shrine seemed suitable. It loomed over the only pathway and no one could miss it. On the morning after the lecture, he had taken Daisy to show her the place he had selected. The shrine was set in a grove of ancient trees, with a small dome and spire, greying with weather. They were going round it inspecting.

Daisy was satisfied with this location, and cried ecstatically, ' This wall seems to have been built for our message!' She turned to Raman and said, 'You know, here we should also have a pictorial medium rather than just words. A father and a mother and just one bright and healthy child with the caption, "With just one, we will be happier." '

Raman could not help asking, 'One? You have said two in other places. Why this reduction here?'

'Oh, this village is different,' she said. 'With the monsoon and other things, the problems here are very peculiar. If I could have my way, I would be prepared to suggest no births in this village for the next five years. The caption to say, "Just the two of us shall remain happy forever without the nuisance of children," but we cannot go so far.' She laughed gravely at her own joke, checked herself halfway through it, and said, 'We must be serious about it, no time to joke, no joking matter.'

Raman felt happy at the effect he had produced. Why shouldn't we also laugh a little while preventing births? Thank God, she is only concerned with births and not death. Otherwise she'll be pestering Yama to take away more people each day, he reflected.

Unnoticed by them, at this moment another person had joined their company. He silently followed Daisy and Raman and closely watched their talks and discussions. As they were studying the blank wall for its possibilities, the new addition to the company silently slid forward and addressed Daisy: 'Why are you gazing on this wall?' She was taken aback, and stepped away as if attacked personally. He said, 'Every brick of this wall and every inch of it was built by me and belongs to me.'

'Oh!' was all that Daisy could say in answer.

Raman said, 'Don't joke, is it true?'

Someone in the crowd that had, unnoticed, gathered around, said, 'Yes, it's true. He dug the earth, made bricks and burnt them, and built this side-wall, little by little. He is more than a hundred years old.'

The old man was pleased at this recognition. He had a loudspeaker voice and wore nothing more than a brown loin-cloth. 'I built this temple and installed the Goddess of Plenty, long before anyone came here and built these houses. The Goddess came to me in a dream and commanded and I made it my mission in life. For a hundred miles around there is no temple like this. Barren women come and pray here for three days, and conceive within thirty days.'

Daisy looked shocked. This was going to prove the antithesis of all her mission, defeat her entire business in life.

Raman's sense of irony was touched: 'We will have to look for another place quickly. Let's leave.'

Before they could decide on it, the old man said in a trumpeting voice: 'Our shastras say that the more children in a home, the more blessed it becomes. Do you want to dispute it?'

Daisy, not having prepared herself for facing such a challenge, blinked uncertainly. Raman came to her rescue and said, 'No, no, how can anyone dispute the shastras?'

'And yet this woman has been propagating sinful practices. I heard a report of what she said. Did she not refer to the priest of the temple? I am the priest. Has this woman anything to say now?'

Daisy said, 'I didn't mean anything bad. I just said that they should ask you for an explanation of the miracle.'

Raman said, 'Don't talk to him, let us go.' But the old man said, 'I know everything that goes on for a hundred miles around, though it's a hundred years since I stepped outside my temple. I know what goes on everywhere and in everyone's mind. I sent my subtle self to your meeting yesterday. I know all that you said. Be careful, you evil women, don't tamper with God's designs. He will strike you dead if you attempt that.' He had a white flowing beard and looked like the messenger of disaster.

Those in the crowd said, 'He can see what goes on even in Delhi!' Another person said, 'He can talk to plants and mountains and birds and animals and they all obey him. He knows past, present, and future . . .' No one gave Daisy a chance to speak. The hermit himself said, 'Would you like to know your future?' looking searchingly at Daisy.

'No,' she said point-blank.

Then he said, 'I'll tell you your past.' Raman rather enjoyed her predicament – all along she had been the positive, leading figure in any group. It was good to see her on the defensive. The hermit suddenly said, 'Mention a number . . .'

'Why?' she asked.

'From that number, I can read your past, where you come from and so forth.' Raman felt that here was one chance of solving several mysteries, and awaited the outcome with interest. The hermit suddenly said, 'Or mention a colour if you don't know any number.'

'No,' she said once again, blushing.

The hermit looked at her mischievously. 'Well, that jacket you are wearing, what colour is it?'

She looked at herself and spurned to give an answer.

Others murmured, 'It's blue, grey, brown.'

'Each of you sees it in a different colour, but I can see it with the eyes of the lady. It's yellow. And that's enough for me. Yellow . . . yellow . . .' He shut his eyes and murmured, 'It's the colour of a particular kind of bell flower – not generally known. It's rare and special. So is your life. You ran away from home, without telling anyone, when you were twelve years old. Your father and mother searched for you, poor things! After months, traced you.' He shut his eyes for a moment and said, 'I see a seashore, waves, huts . . .'

Daisy looked somewhat shaken, turned to Raman, and said, 'We will go now,' and abruptly moved off. She remained silent a moment and added, 'I don't think that he'll let us use his wall.'

'That's certain,' Raman said. 'He may add his own message to the barren women over ours. That may create confusion.'

The crowd still followed. Someone kept saying, 'He can talk to birds and animals; he is a yogi . . .'

'He is one hundred years old . . .'

'A hundred long ago, now must be more.'

'See how strong he is!'

'He built this temple with his own hands. He can go anywhere at will.'

'I know all that,' Daisy said, irritated. 'It's all been repeated,' not liking the worshipful attitude of this public. She reached the teacher's house and went in unceremoniously. Raman took his seat on the *pyol*. The crowd still hung around the steps of the house and overflowed into the street. The teacher had gone out to a market near by and come back laden with vegetables, fruits, and provisions. He was planning a feast for his guests before their departure next day. He was panting with the load on his back. His wife came outside and took charge of his shopping bag and went in. They had a brief discussion over the prices paid and his selections, in whispers.

'The doctor is taking rest,' the teacher's wife announced.

'Yes, we have been walking about since day-break,' said Raman.

The teacher looked at the crowd and said, 'There is nothing more now. You may all go. As you have just heard, the doctor is resting.' The crowd turned back and dispersed down the street.

Raman mentioned, 'We met that old man in the other temple.'

The teacher said, 'Oh, him! He is a yogi, not afraid of anyone in the world.'

'Is he a real yogi?' asked Raman.

The teacher said, 'We have learnt to leave him alone. It's not safe to make an enemy of him. He can be helpful. He has all sorts of powers. Lives on nothing, says he. Nourishes himself from air. It is not good to argue with him. He is a quarrelsome man and commands powers.'

'I selected his wall . . .'

'Don't go near it,' said the teacher. 'If you had told me . . .'

Raman said, 'Don't remind her of the incident. She is rather upset.'

After lunch everybody retired for an hour's siesta. With the sun beating down fiercely, the village withdrew into itself. Dogs lay curled up in the shade of trees or buildings, cattle lay down on the ground, chewing the cud, crows cawed from the branches of trees desultorily. The pulley over the village well ceased to creak. Raman sat on the *pyol* after lunch. Daisy had retired to her room until the evening. Her next engagement would be a talk to a gathering of women in the school-hall. The *pyol* was shady, and the teacher stretched himself across and invited Raman to do likewise. Raman sat up beside the teacher for a little while, and when he found him half-drowsy, said, 'Well, I'll have to select another spot. We have not much time left. If the lady asks, tell her I'm out and will be back soon. Let her rest.'

He put his sandals on and stepped out of the house. Writing on the wall was impractical in this village as most of the houses were built closely packed and the end-walls were not suitably placed. The cave-temple outer wall was most desirable in every way, and if he could cajole the hermit to let it out for a rent, it would help. Otherwise they'd have to use the rockface on the northern side where one would have to go up a scaffolding to write. He had taken the precaution of not mentioning that place to Daisy – otherwise she'd ask him to put up a scaffolding and climb it with a brush, like a house-painter. He felt indignant. He was straying away, drawn by this fair creature, from his legitimate normal activity – if he was to go up a scaffolding, that'd be the end of all his ideals and independence, he'd lose the respect of his fellow-men. No doubt he was being paid liberally, but that was not the main thing. He had always written his boards on the sands behind his house; after the present assignment, he must suggest some other device for wall messages. He'd write on wood or canvas and stick them up, but this kind of wall-writing, no, no. He went past the coconut grove, so full of shade that one would hardly remember the hot sun baking the streets of the village. He went along the path leading to the mountains, up an avenue of tamarind trees to the cave temple. He walked around it, only one wall, a sheer wall with a smooth face; the rest of it was ragged and covered with the dust of decades, and unapproachable through the thicket grown around it. He wished he had spent more time with the old crank, who had excited his curiosity. He could, perhaps, fill in a great deal of the blanks in his knowledge of Daisy's life, and if he could be coaxed to rent his wall, it would save a lot of trouble, otherwise Daisy was sure to feel frustrated and fret about it. Moreover Raman was fascinated by the fantastic claims made by this superman, and the simple faith of the citizens of this place. As he stood there, ruminating, the hermit came out of his cave and glared at him. Raman made a low obeisance, folded his palms together to exhibit his friendliness and reverence for the old man. 'So you are back here!' the old man cried. 'The third time I see you here, take care . . . take care!'

'I mean no harm,' Raman said meekly. 'I just wanted to see you, that is all.'

'What business have you here unless you wish to cure your wife's barrenness?'

'I am not married,' Raman said.

'Don't I know it?' the other cried. 'Perhaps a mistress who wishes to remain barren and preach the same philosophy to the whole world . . . He! He!' he giggled viciously.

'I wish to see this temple,' Raman said unceremoniously.

'Why?' asked the man. 'What is your business here?'

Raman said, 'Just to hear you discourse on life and other matters. You are like an ancient rishi, a rare person to meet. When one meets a great soul and hears his talk, one attains merit, so say the shastras!'

This pleased the old man unexpectedly. His face relaxed; he said, 'Follow me. I can depend upon wild animals to listen to reason, but I am not so sure of influencing human beings.' He led him around to the mouth of the cave, which had a low, circular entrance, and Raman had to stoop his way in while the old man wriggled in as if he were a snake entering its hole. 'You see, sometimes an old tiger turned "maneater" comes around. He would wait behind a shrub and carry away the villagers. So many cowherds have disappeared and also woodcutters and stonemasons. The doors of all the homes are shut and nobody will come out when a "maneater" is on the prowl. Life comes to a standstill. The village becomes dead. At such times, I am the only human being to be seen outside. Once I found a tiger hiding himself in these thickets. He licked his tongue when he heard a human being approaching, but when he saw who it was, he knew he had lost the game. I addressed the Universal Soul directly: "O Soul, take that clumsy tiger body of yours off and don't come and trouble the people any more," and the tiger bolted away in shame. At another time I told the wild elephant who was ransacking the gardens and fields, "Hey, Gaja! Get away, otherwise I will bring down on you the chastisement of Gajendra, the Lord of all Elephants in the Heaven." I can argue cobras out of my way. You must talk to them. They never talk back. But say something to a human being, he will argue.'

'No one dare argue with you,' Raman said, much to the delight of the old man.

The roof was very low. A narrow corridor went around the shrine and an extra room at a cellar level was the living room of this hermit. An oil-lamp kept burning inside the sanctum and a stone image was visible faintly in that wick-light.

'Go near and see the Goddess. Don't fear,' he commanded. ' That Goddess is not meant only for women, remember. Even men can worship her if they want to be determined and brave and achieve their objects.'

'But you never mentioned about men, all along. Only women were allowed, I thought.'

'Because they are more earnest about getting the blessing of this Goddess. He! He! He! Men don't mind remaining imbeciles. Go, go, go near the Goddess and pray for whatever blessing you seek; I'd not normally allow men to enter this temple, but you seem to be an honest fellow. You may go near the Goddess; go and watch the power in her eyes and you will be the better for it.' Raman stooped through two portals and stood before the image, which was decorated with flowers. The fragrance of flowers and incense hung in the air. The old man stood at the farthest end and cried, 'Don't stand moping. Pray to her and express your wish.' Raman felt overwhelmed by the man's authority. Still he could not tell him that his aim in life was to establish the Age of Reason, and he could think of no boons to ask of a Goddess. Yet he noticed the benevolence in the eyes of the image and a desire to impart grace. He just mumbled, 'May Daisy be mine without further delay. I can't live without her.'

He turned round and went back to the old man, who grinned at him knowingly. 'Did you notice the single flower that fell down from the crown? That's an omen – which means success, but trouble before and after. Did you see that that flower rolled down to her arm first and then the feet and then on to the floor? It it had rested on her arm or lap, it'd have meant a good answer for your prayer. Don't give up trying, don't hesitate, you will gain nothing if you brood and mope and waste your time. Mopers will get nowhere in life . . . Come here and sit down.' Raman obeyed him implicitly and squatted on the floor facing him. The hermit sat, completely coiling up his long legs; his fluffy beard fluttered in a draft of air that seemed to be stealing in from somewhere.

Raman made bold to ask, 'Tell me about her.'

The old man shook his head. 'Not when she is not present.'

Raman cried, 'I know nothing about her and she won't talk about her past.' The man smiled in a sinister manner. 'Except what you said . . . that she had left home when young.'

'That's all you need to know. And then didn't I say where she was found?'

'I don't even know if she is married or not.'

'What does it matter? Do you see a husband around?'

'No. But he may turn up.'

The old man laughed heartily. 'H'm. Good reason to worry.'

Raman felt he was making a fool of himself. There was something in this temple which cowed one and made one prattle. He wanted to assert himself and changed the subject, something to put the other man on the defensive. 'And so the women who want to pray stay here?'

'What's that to you?' asked the old man with a sudden aggressiveness. Raman looked about the semi-dark and lonely hall significantly. The old man said, 'This Goddess helps women who are childless. Go away, man, you are a bad fellow with evil thoughts.'

Raman got up, noticing the old man's change of mood. He seemed to be so undependable. Raman said with a sudden firmness, 'Will you permit me to write on your outer wall our "No children" message?'

'No,' said the old man with equal firmness. 'You evil-minded man. No, no, no, you get out of here first.' He dramatically held a finger towards the exit, and Raman slunk out shame-faced.

They realized that the village walls were unsuitable for inscribing on, and decided to leave it over for the present, confining themselves to other forms of propaganda. Daisy wanted to know if any of the rockfaces would be suitable, but Raman became evasive and suggested that they could consider any fresh investigation only after the monsoon. 'And let us hope that at least from next year they will take care of their birth-rates.'

Daisy shot a look at him as if to gauge how serious he was. Raman set his face into a grim seriousness. They were all sitting on the teacher's *pyol* ready for departure. They had spent three days in this camp and were partially satisfied with the work done. The hermit's attack still rankled in her mind. 'I fear we have to contend against that man's propaganda.'

'Let's not talk about him. He understands what goes on everywhere.'

'Why should one be afraid?' Daisy asked. 'We are all working for a cause that's of national importance. I wish I could talk to him. I am sure he would be convinced.'

'I'm telling you that he knows all that is said and done anywhere. Not necessary to go and speak to him again.'

'Oh, master, you must rise above all such superstitious fears.'

'Let us talk of something else,' said the teacher, and rose to leave. They had to walk back the three or four miles to the highway and hope for a bus or a lorry to pick them up. The teacher was to escort them up to a point. His wife had packed rice, curds, vegetables, and other eatables for their lunch and dinner. She had grown attached to Daisy, and became sentimental at her departure. There were tears in her eyes, and her children stood around rather overawed by the scene of parting.

Daisy looked at them critically. 'Don't suck your thumb, take it out, otherwise you will stammer,' she said to one. To another one she said, 'Stand erect, don't slouch.' She turned to their mother and added, 'Correct posture is important. Children must be taught all this early in life.' She was a born mentor, could not leave others alone, children had better not be born, but if born, must take their thumbs out of their mouths and avoid slouching. She somehow did not have any advice to offer the elders. She just looked at them as if to say, Behave yourselves, and bade the family good-bye. Raman never took his eyes off her even for a moment, fascinated by her positive manner and talk. He smiled and muttered his thanks in the midst of this babble, addressing himself to no one in particular, and stepped out. The teacher led the way mutely. A few villagers stood aside to watch them go and murmured among themselves, 'The doctor is leaving,' almost with relief. They would not have to feel apologetic any more for being fathers and mothers.

She had many words of advice, cautions, and precautions for the teacher when they reached the main road on the hill. The teacher looked intimidated by Daisy's manner. She spoke as if he'd be held responsible for any birth occurring in the village. 'We will be delayed by the onset of the monsoon, but we will definitely be here as soon as possible after that,' she said half-menacingly. Raman looked at the teacher as if wondering how this frail man was going to prevent the seven-hundred-odd men and women from ever coming together. What a task she was levying on this poor man!

They waited in the shade of a tree at the cross-roads. The teacher said, 'The bus should be here any minute.' He repeated this message every few minutes in order to keep up the morale. Daisy sat on a boulder as if it were a throne. Her imperious manner both charmed and frightened Raman. In her previous incarnation, she must have been Queen Victoria, or in a still earlier incarnation Rani Jhansi, the warrior queen of Indian history. The air throbbed with the sound of a distant bus. A family of monkeys on a fig tree a few feet away chattered, the youngest one performing trapeze acts holding on to his mother's dangling tail, while she combed the male monkey's back for lice with her finger-nails. The family looked down on the human beings assembled below. The teacher hung about uncertainly. He was showing slight signs of restlessness. Perhaps he wanted to get back home, and not wait indefinitely for the bus, but was afraid to say so. The company was becoming dull and strained. Raman moved about aimlessly. He was getting tired of watching the shimmering horizon; his aesthetic sensibilities were deadened so that he was not particularly thrilled by the sky and the mountain and the valleys and gorges or the ravines – he sighed for the bustle and noise of the Ellaman Street corner, around the Chettiar shop. He strolled up to the fig tree to watch the monkeys. He went back to Daisy as she sat on her throne with her thoughts, while the teacher stood a little apart, respectfully, like a courtier. Raman watched the teacher's face; it was evident that he had been talked to on a variety of subjects, and now a phase of silence seemed to prevail. Raman breezily declared, 'Did you see the monkeys on the tree?' She looked up without much interest in the direction and looked down again, saying nothing. Raman felt an impulse to make a humorous comment about the family matters of monkeys, but could not pluck up enough courage to do so. He noted that she looked rather dry and her lips looked powdery, ashen, and as if they would crack like the ground in a sun-baked desert. He suggested solicitously, 'A drink of water?'

'Not yet,' she said. 'We have to use it sparingly.'

'Might we not finish our lunch?'

'I'm more keen on a bus,' she said with a condescending humour, feeling perhaps it was time to relax. Somehow today she seemed to have decided to conduct herself in a queenly manner in the presence of the teacher, who looked crushed and submissive; although on the *pyol* of his house he had ventured to be so argumentative. Raman thought, Every person is so much a part of his background – take him away from it and he becomes limp and featureless.

'Where is the bus we heard?'

'Must have been a lorry going down somewhere else,' replied the teacher.

'You have no idea of the bus timings?'

'Some days they are irregular and don't come at all.'

'And so?'

He blinked as if caught in a trap. 'If the bus is delayed today – it should have arrived by this time. A bullock-cart may be found. I'll go down the lower road and get one from the village. They generally avoid this road because of its gradient.' At a nod from Daisy, he slipped down the slope, and soon disappeared round a bend. Raman again suggested lunch. They opened one packet and ate in silence. The second packet was for the night. A drink of water after it, and he felt refreshed, and he also noticed that Daisy looked better now.

Eventually, around four o'clock, the bullock-cart rumbled in from somewhere and the teacher jumped out of it. 'Teacher, you must be starving, we've had our lunch,' said Daisy.

'I have eaten at the village.'

It was a mat-covered wagon, drawn by a white bull with small bells around its neck which jingled when it moved. A little time was spent in arguing about the fare. The teacher said, 'I have fixed him for four rupees, and he will take you to Koppal, where you can take the bus for Malgudi Town.'

The cart-driver, an old man who continuously swore at the animal, stared at his passengers while they climbed into the cart, and said, 'I always like to take in newlyweds. If it had been someone else, I'd not have accepted this trip for less than six rupees, not a paisa less. The price of hay is going up. I am not the sort of person who'll let his animals feed on roadside trees. That way you can shorten the beast's life – "beast" – did I say "beast"? I don't like the word, it's a cruel and insulting word for a living creature. I smashed the eyes and nose of a fellow who called me "beast" once. Today I'm like this, but when I was young, oh, God, it looks like another Janma, and yet it's so clear before my mind like a picture, my son was so little that he sat on my lap and held the reins and drove the bullocks himself; what a noise he'd make with his tongue, that'd make the animals gallop, I tell you. So small, just the size of the whip-handle but he could drive the bulls mad. But I didn't want him to be a driver of bulls. I wanted him to study, the teacher in our village said that he would be the most intelligent boy in the country . . .' The old man went on talking all through the journey, to the tune of the jingling bells.

Raman occasionally interrupted whenever he felt that the old man should give rest to his vocal cords. 'Where is that son now?'

'I don't know,' the old man said. 'He went away to the town and worked in a factory, and won't remember us any more.' Raman wanted to inquire if he was married and how many children and so forth, but he avoided the topic as he did not like to stir up Daisy. The old man, just as an encouragement to the young couple, expatiated on the virtues of married life. He said, 'I lost four wives, but never remained without one at any time. I tell you, there is no greater joy than a wife for a man. My fifth wife –'

'How many children?' Raman asked, rather involuntarily.

'Not more than four from each – God gives us children, and who are we to say no to Him?' Luckily, Daisy was in a drowse leaning back on the mat-covered side, and Raman managed to change the topic.

At some point Daisy woke up to inquire, 'We are still on the road? What time is it?'

'Six.'

'Let us get into a bus, if one comes up.'

'No bus here,' the cartman added. 'What's wrong with this

carriage? Are you unhappy in it?' They were not. There was a layer of straw and a carpet over it – very cosy – and it had an agreeably musty smell about it. They went down the mountain road and finally reached the highway from the Mempi Hills leading to the towns in the plains, passing through a fine avenue lined with palmyra and coconut trees. The ride in the cart seemed to create an intimacy; with so little space between them, the barriers between them seemed to be falling. Daisy became more communicative. Raman realized that her communicative phase was reviving now and made the best of it. She presented a stiff, frozen personality when performing a public duty or talking to people like the teacher; once that was over, her normal charm returned, the kind of face she had presented when she opened the door for him at Number Seven, Third Cross. He loved her now unreservedly. When he stole a glance at her, his heart beat fast. He did a little introspection and said to himself, It's the same person I saw in the village, and have been seeing here and there, the tight lipped monomaniac, but now what is it in her that is sending my heart racing? Silly . . . But he could not help it. He wanted to go on talking to her, go on hearing her voice; but the only topics she could appreciate were birth-control, population, and allied subjects! There was no use talking to her about weather, political crises, or economic theories. She just turned a deaf ear to all other themes! No use involving her in a conversation even about music, or culture, or philosophy. She either did not care for such things, or deliberately hardened herself against them, in order, probably, not to lose her concentration. She was like a yogi with his eyes fixed on the centre of his nose, seeing nothing else in life. Didn't matter. Nothing mattered as long as she was there, and remained herself, with that aroma of some strange herb, perhaps some little hair oil – but he had never seen her grooming herself, never seen her spending any time before a mirror. But then, he reflected, how could he know what she did when she shut the door of whatever room she might happen to be in at the moment? His imagination wallowed in speculation of all that she might do in the privacy of a room, dressing or washing.

At some point, the cartman was good enough to ask him to move back a little, to the centre of the carriage, in order to keep the balance on the axle; otherwise the cart tilted forward. It was a welcome suggestion, as it placed him nearer to her fragrant presence. He desperately wanted to establish union with her, at least verbally. He realized that the best policy would be to adopt the look of a simple-minded inquirer seeking illumination. She would definitely love to behave like a guru for such a disciple. As a first step this would be excellent. Once it was established, he could go on to the next stage. It'd not be necessary to stay on birth-control forever. He could gradually touch upon other matters, he could reveal himself in all his nakedness. Nakedness? Why did this word creep in now, he wondered. It was inevitable under the present circumstances. No one could prohibit him the use of that expression. Presently, assuming a most innocent look he remarked, 'There are some questions about the use of certain types of contraceptives which I have never understood.'

She sat up, coming out of a torpor induced by the movement of the carriage, and asked over the din of the wheels, 'What in particular is it that you want to know about?'

He didn't expect to be cross-examined thus. He mumbled, 'I always wanted to know whenever you talked about it, but I didn't wish to interrupt you.'

'That's all right. What is it you want to know?'

He had now to come out with it, and mentioned some vague point, which sounded so naïve that she began to laugh. First time in many days. She laughed so loudly that the cartman turned round, nodded his head knowingly, and turned away to face the road once again.

She said, 'I hope you know enough physiology to follow any explanation?'

Raman felt caught, he did not know whether to say yes or no. If he said yes she might begin to think ill of him, or if he said no she might take him to be a simpleton without any knowledge about the world. This was the lesser of the two evils.

'Well, how could I be expected to know so much of this subject? Of course, some amount of physiology learnt in the classroom long ago and also some general knowledge picked up here and there. But it's somewhat limited, naturally.'

'Are you so innocent?' she asked.

He wondered if he should begin a confession! How that tall college girl of his class once enticed him, when they had gone on a holiday camp, to sneak behind an abandoned shed, while others were busy. And then . . . only two other instances, mere calf-love and infructuous attempts at love-making, nothing of consequence or importance. Best not to speak of it now. She might lose trust in him. He pretended total ignorance of the entire subject; giving himself a saintly aura on the whole.

She began a preamble: 'That's the reason I feel strongly that sex-education must be given from the kindergarten stage. Otherwise so much ignorance and taboo – it's led to the present state of affairs. I hope you at least know that it's the easiest thing to produce a baby –'

'Yes, of course, but not always practical,' he said, while she went on – 'the more difficult thing is to stop one from coming. This is the point which I wish to emphasize everywhere, in every nook and corner of the country, dinning it into every citizen, old and young.' She seemed all of a sudden to be getting into the spirit of public speaking, forgetting that she was cooped up in a bullock-cart with an audience of one or perhaps two, if the cart-driver was to be included. She went into great detail, without the slightest inhibition, about the course a recalcitrant sperm took and the strategy to halt its journey. She touched upon various aspects of contraception, spoke with such zeal that Raman began to wonder what freakish experience or trauma might be responsible for this sort of unmitigated antagonism to conception. He had heard all this before, over and over again, when she addressed village audiences; but now this was a sort of command performance in this narrow closed space, all alone on the highway. It thrilled him and gave him vicarious satisfaction.

It was seven o'clock. They were planning to catch the town bus leaving Koppal at eight for Malgudi. They had been journeying for over three hours now. The cartman suddenly pulled up crying. 'Damned, accursed thing.' The bullock had stumbled and hurt its leg. The cartman got off his seat and went up to examine the injury. The passengers also got down. The old man looked both forlorn and angry. He hit the animal on its haunches with the handle of the whip, and said, 'I knew it'd do this sort of thing.'

'What has happened?' they asked anxiously.

'He has hurt himself – the fool didn't use his eyes, and has injured his leg. Should not a sensible animal use his eyes and see what's ahead, if a pit or furrow is there? The son-of-a . . .' He made allusions to the mixed-up, ill-begotten progenitors of this creature. He quickly unyoked the animal, took its foreleg in his hand, and examined it with tender care – for all the foul references in his speech. He was almost in tears as he said, 'He can't pull any more.' He stood brooding for a moment as to what he should do.

Daisy and Raman looked rather worried. 'So what do we do?' they asked in unison.

'I'll take him to the village over there, where he will have an application of medicinal leaves . . .'

To Raman the cartman seemed more preoccupied with the animal's leg than with their fate. He went on elaborating about the medicament for the animal until Raman was forced to inquire, 'What are we to do?'

'Stay here or come with me. I'll get another bull to go forward. I promised to take you to Koppal – I'll keep the promise, don't worry.'

'How far away is the village?'

'My nephew lives there and he will help me.'

'Good. How far away is it, I asked.'

'How do I know? I don't carry a measuring rod. I can go there, and I promise that I'll be back and take you onward. I have promised you that I'll take you to Koppal. I'll take you there. Don't worry. This place is safe, no robbers or evil spirits, and I'll be back. The place is safe. You have there a nice bed of straw with a carpet. Eat your food and sleep peacefully. I'll be back. I have travelled down this road hundreds of times in my life . . . This place is as safe as your bedroom. Eat and sleep peacefully. I'll come back with a good yoke.' He dragged the cart under a tree and, with many suggestive hints to the newlywed couple, was gone with his animal. The jingling of its bell came from a distance. A half-moon appeared in the sky.

They became self-conscious at being left alone and looked at each other in embarrassment. This sudden isolation seemed to place a moral burden on them both. For a moment Raman welcomed the opportunity, but actually felt nervous. He had had no notion how important the old cart-driver's presence had been. They stood about rather uncertainly. A fear came over him that any move on his part was likely to be misunderstood. He said, 'A nice breeze blowing.'

'Yes,' Daisy said, without any special spirit.

He looked up heavenward and declared, 'A half-moon, rather pretty, isn't it?'

'Yes, it is.'

'A full moon would have been glorious, don't you think?'

'Yes,' she said, still looking in the direction in which the old man had departed – he had suddenly plunged into a bush and gone off cross-country. 'What a fellow to leave us stranded like this!' she said in a tone of slight horror.

'Oh, he will come back, can't have gone very far. Are you afraid?'

She shook her head rather contemptuously. 'It is not that. I am used to worse situations in life, but he should have told us where he was going.'

'Perhaps we could abandon this cart and walk to the nearest village. It would serve him right.' She remained silent over this solution. He said, 'Would you say that you are tired or can you walk? . . . Let us pick up our things and leave this place.' He looked at his watch rather purposelessly, and muttered, Half past something or other. She ignored his suggestion, and looked about for her usual throne in such places, could find none, flashed her torch on the ground, and, finding it clear, sat down. ' The important thing is to see that there are no reptiles around,' he commented, and followed suit, sitting a little away from her. It was hard for him to decide what distance he should keep from her; with a third person in the company he could nestle close to her as in the waggon, but now he wanted to avoid the slightest trace of a suspicious movement. He shifted and moved away and sat where it would not be too near to create a bad impression or too far if she preferred his company. After an approximate calculation, he got up again and took another seat, as if it were a game of human chess – the sort of game that the Mughal emperors played with human chessmen on marble squares in medieval times. He decided that if she moved even a hair's breadth closer to where he sat, he would take it as a signal for him to make a move, and ultimately there should be no space between them whatever. He noticed that she had now got into her non-speaking phase and he would have to respect her silence.

They sat thus for a while, and then he said abruptly, 'Past eight. Let me serve your dinner.' She acquiesced. He rose and went back to the cart and took out their little hamper of food. He gave it over to her, placed before her the water bottle too, and waited for her to begin. She opened the food container, tore a banana leaf in two, heaped on one a portion of rice, and held it to him. He said, 'It is kind of you,' and ate in silence. Vague sounds of night birds and insects unseen stirred the air. It was a first night between an awkward couple. Perhaps so in his imagination. After the food she held out to him a cup of water. We are a well-matched couple – how well she looks after me! he reflected. What would I not give to know what is passing in her mind? The crux of the problem is not now, it is what comes after the dinner.

After the rice and a drink of water, her mood seemed to improve and she became communicative. 'Quite a volume of correspondence must have piled up on my desk, and it is tackling the letters that really worries me. I don't mind any amount of field-work.'

'Don't hesitate if I can be of any help,' he said.

'Well, well, I can manage it; I have always managed these things myself. I am not cut out for desk work, I think.'

'Oh, no, I would not agree with you. Well, you are so effective when you are dealing officially – as I found out when I brought the first sign-board for your office the other day. It seems so long ago!' he said wistfully.

'Actually twelve weeks ago, not longer . . .' she said with precision.

He smiled uncomfortably. 'I feel as if we had known each other several Janmas,' he said rather plaintively.

'It is imagination really,' she said. 'Do you believe in reincarnation?'

He wanted to make sure that he should have the right answer for her and asked, 'Do you?'

'No,' she said bluntly.

He replied, ' There are some people who believe in it, and some others who don't. Opinion is divided –'

'I am asking what you think.'

'Oh, I am so busy all the time, no time to brood over such questions. Well, perhaps when I sit calmly in retirement, I shall be about to sort out these questions.' Now he said rather gallantly, 'You have been walking and straining yourself since the morning. Please climb into that carriage and sleep if you like. I will remain outside and keep a watch. The cartman has lowered the front of the cart to that culvert so that it doesn't slope down, but keeps level.'

'You have also been quite active the whole day – must be as tired. Why don't you get in and sleep first? I will stay out and watch.'

'Oh, no,' he said, 'it is a man's duty. I will stay out, you get in.'

She said after considering the question, 'Let us see . . .' Briskly she went up to the cart, brought out a roll of carpet and a pillow. 'You will have to sleep under the carriage, it will be cosy, only remember not to knock your head when you rise,' and they both laughed. She added, 'Some people cannot sleep with the sky open above them . . .'

'I am one such, how did you guess . . .'

She knelt down, spread the carpet for him with a sprinkling of straw under it, placed the pillow, and made his bed. Raman felt tender and grateful. He put his head into the carriage to arrange her bed reciprocally, flashed his torch in, and smoothed out the straw and the little carpet the cartman had placed there. They washed the vessels with a little water and packed them away. 'We may at least rest until the cart-driver returns. I hope it won't be difficult to wake you up.' Raman helped her to climb into her bed, hung about a little, and crept under the carriage.

The moonlight, stars, the cool breeze – everything seemed to affect his equanimity. He lay tossing on his bed of straw, looking up longingly at the bottom of the cart. He debated within himself whether to dash up, seize her, and behave like Rudolph Valentino in *The Sheik*, which he had seen as a student. Women liked an aggressive lover – so said the novelists. He recollected piecemeal all her words of the last three weeks – those three weeks had brought them closer than anyone could hope for in three years. A secret life seemed to have developed between them. When they had travelled jogging in the bullock-cart, in the narrow space, they often rubbed shoulders and their knees touched. Once when the cart bumped rather roughly over a track, they were flung against each other. Once or twice, he thrust his arm forward and tried to touch her; she fended him off unobtrusively. His whole being was convulsed with waves of desire now. He said to himself, I adore her, but this silly tension that's rising within me must be quelled. I should, perhaps, meditate on the Third Eye of Shiva, by opening which he reduced the God of Love to ashes, and, perhaps, achieved what we nowadays call sublimation. He brooded and projected himself ahead. He would just slip in and hold her down if she resisted. And then she'd become pregnant. That'd make her run to him for support. Good thing, too. Send away Aunt to her cousin's house in the village. Daisy would live in Ellaman Street with their child – nice and normal; but if she gave birth to twins – there were many cases of twins these days – they'd probably sack her for unprofessional conduct. That'd be a good thing too. She would come to depend upon him completely and he would protect her and give her a good life. Only he'd have to run around a little more and secure more orders; that would be managed. Everything seemed to be working out well, fitting into a preordained scheme, what could be more normal than, with a man and woman lying under the stars separated by an artificial man-made barrier, smashing that barrier in order to spend the night in a proper embrace? He peeped out – twinkling stars and the half moon on the horizon about to set. He felt one was wasting one's opportunities lying on hard ground. He softly crawled out, raised himself, stood at the mouth of the waggon. He hesitated for a moment whether to call her in a soft whisper and then proceed or – it seemed irrelevant to go through all such formality; this was no time for hesitation. This was a god-given moment meant for action. Man must live for the moment and extract its essence. Every minute becomes a yesterday, and is lost forever. 'Today is tomorrow's yesterday.' He heaved himself up and slid into the waggon blindly. He saw nothing, forgot his surroundings, his only aim being to seize his prey, whatever the consequences. The future was a silly, insignificant notion and meant nothing. Everything that he felt impelled to do seemed to him perfectly justifiable. He whispered: 'Don't fear, it's only me, my sweetheart. Don't torment me,' and flung his arm around where she would be.

But she was not there. The carpet was still warm. He ran his hand up and down so as to know if she had hidden herself under a layer of straw. Only his fingers felt and picked up a piece of garment of soft material, and he seized it as if it were a booty. Where is she, while her undergarment is here? The shameless creature! Where is she gone? Eloped with someone for the night, without impediments!

His tension suddenly relaxed. He felt it absurd to be holding this thing in his fist, and put it back. He called, 'Daisy! Daisy!' He got out and ran hither and thither calling her. Began to feel worried. Or could it be she was Mohini, who tempted men and fooled them? He quietly went back to his own carpet under the cart.

In the morning he crawled out from under the carriage. The cartman had come, and cheerily explained, 'I woke up my nephew, it took me half the night to get to him, and then the rascal would not get up. I had to bang on his door till he came out and attended to me.' He asked, 'Slept well?'

'Yes, yes.'

The cartman forbore to look into the waggon where the lady was supposed to be asleep. After waiting for a little time: 'If the lady wakes up, I can yoke the bullock and start out.' The birds were chirping and creating a din on the branches of trees. 'Where is the lady?' he asked suddenly. Raman wondered what to say. The cart-driver added, 'Must have gone to the well. There is one near by – quite shallow; but the water is very sweet. Have you washed?'

'Presently,' Raman said with casual ease. 'After she comes,' secretly wondering if he was destined to see her again but speaking in a tone as if he were waiting at the door of a bathroom. Suppose she had stumbled into that well? 'How far away is the well?' he asked.

'Just beyond that tamarind tree, that's why I unyoked here. I thought you might have noticed it.'

'Yes, of course. She mentioned the well, but I didn't look for it yet.' He sounded like a seasoned husband who left everything to a wife's management and completely depended upon her, including the directions for a morning wash.

Raman felt light in the head, the aftermath of the upsurge of love, his eventual moral collapse (as it seemed), and the frustration of it all.

'Women observe these things first,' said the cartman. They saw Daisy approaching from beyond the tamarind tree. She had tidied herself up at the well, and looked quite bright. A few drops of water still glistened on her forehead. She had been wiping her face with the end of her sari. As she came up, he wanted to say, I know you are wearing nothing inside. We'll now leave you to put your clothes back on your good self.

The cartman said, 'I'll give this animal a drink of water and then we may go . . .'

Raman did not spend much time looking at her. He followed the cart-driver, saying, 'I'll have a wash at the well.'

'If you are brisk, you can catch the bus at Koppal. At the bus-stand, there is a coffee-shop. The lady must be hungry. I'll take you there as fast as possible.'

The cartman drove his bullock towards the well. Raman followed him mutely, leaving Daisy without a word or a glance in her direction. He was aware of the flash of her grey-coloured sari from a corner of his eye. He felt that perhaps she expected him to say something, a greeting, explanation or something, and his going off must surprise her, he thought. But he did not care how she felt. He had a rage against her for deserting him. She had committed a wrong, as it seemed to him. Was it wrong? he asked, bewildered. Who was in the wrong, actually? He couldn't be sure. If he had succeeded in his desperate aim last night, he might have ended up in prison for rape. In course of time he might have had to be greeting the twins from behind the bars. Some providence had protected him in spite of himself. At this realization, he felt lighter at heart and even vaguely grateful to the girl for taking herself away in good time and thus saving him. No more reference to this; he must forget it completely and wipe it from his memory. He was appalled at the potentialities that lay buried within him. No reference, no reference, he told himself.

In spite of this resolution, when they were again sitting in the waggon on their way to the bus-stand ten miles away, he couldn't help saying the first sentence for the day. 'Thanks for saving me.'

'Yes?' she said.

'From myself,' he added. She made no response. The jingling of the bells of the bullock were the only sound for a while. He inquired gently, 'Where were you?'

'On a branch of the tamarind tree.'

'All night?' he whispered.

'Yes, until the dawn.'

'I am sorry you should have suffered there.'

'Yes, it was not comfortable but protected from the prowling tiger.' For a minute he felt a relief that it was only a tiger that had driven her out. 'You said tiger? How big was it?'

'I heard it scratching the mat under the cart, and when it appeared at the mouth of the carriage, I managed to slip out the other end to the tree . . .'

Raman felt it would be best to observe silence. Then he asked suddenly, 'When did you learn tree climbing?'

'We used to play Gorilla when I was young; whoever becomes a Gorilla must climb a tree and stay there. We used to play this for hours day after day, and that's been helpful. I now realize the meaning of the proverb, "When you are married to the devil, you must be prepared to climb the tamarind tree" – they must have had me in mind.'

'But you are not married,' he ventured to joke.

She was grim when she said, 'They must also have meant the company one keeps.' She looked serious. Raman remained silent.

The cartman, without turning his head, in between two swear-words aimed at his animal asked, 'Did you have a fight?'

'Yes,' Raman said.

'What about?' he asked, looking ahead at the road.

'Oh, you know, this and that . . .'

'I used to thrash my wife when I had drinks in me,' the cartman said. 'But you are educated persons, and you are different.'

It turned out to be a rather grim journey homeward. After her mention of the tiger and the devil, Daisy just withdrew into herself. Raman was abashed to be sitting so close to one whom he had driven up a tamarind tree. What did she mean by this proverb? He had often heard his aunt mention it. Did she think of herself as married to him already? Or did she have any clue as to the thoughts crossing his mind? For a moment he felt happy and relieved that she was perhaps beginning to take him seriously. If so, why this silence? He threw a furtive look at her, and found her gazing at him; it was ridiculous to behave like dumb animals sitting within inches of each other. She looked frozen. Still, a few droplets of water stood along her brow like the jewels in a coronet. He said to break the awkwardness, 'You remind me of Queen Victoria.'

A reckless statement, but he had decided to be reckless. After the drive and pressure that he had felt last night he was resolved not to be submissive and timid, but prove himself her equal in toughness. She should learn to respect him and not treat him as if he were a hanger-on to be spoken to when it pleased her or dropped at other times. The moment of contrition was gone. He had done nothing to feel guilty about – the normal drive of a force which kept the whole world spinning. Nothing to be ashamed of, nothing to be apologetic about. If he had not tried to make use of an opportunity in the normal manner, he would have been considered a worthless sot in some circles. She had no reason to be so grim, as he had done nothing to warrant such an attitude. He had obliged her by wandering like a vagrant with her, putting himself through all kinds of travails, giving up his normal business, friends, and Aunt – what did she mean by this haughty aloofness? He said several times to himself, I have done nothing wrong. He spoke now with some amount of arrogance. 'You will say nothing in reply?'

'I have nothing to say.'

'I have called you Queen Victoria, and you have no comment to make!'

She looked at him coldly and asked, 'What are you trying? Joking, teasing, or worrying me?' Her voice quivered a little and she glared at him.

'I just want to cheer you up, that is all. There is no reason why you should sulk and treat me in this manner. After all, what have I done except to show my . . . my –'

At this point Daisy tapped the cart-driver on his shoulder and said, 'Stop, hey, stop.'

The cart-driver turned round, bewildered.

She insisted, 'I said, "stop." ' He pulled up the reins, and the bullock, which had been trotting, came to a sudden halt. She picked up her little bag, slipped down from the carriage, and ordered the driver, ' Take that man where he wants to go. I am not riding in this any more.'

The cartman smiled. 'How will you get to the bus? It is quite far away.'

'Don't concern yourself with that. Take him, I tell you.'

At this Raman picked up his own bag and stepped out, saying, 'You get in, I will get out and walk.'

The cartman got down from his seat and said, 'Come, come. This won't do. How can you get away from each other when God has put you in wedlock? Impossible. Where are your children? Quarrels and fights such as this are inevitable, and you should not make too much of it. Go back, get along. H'm, get in. You will both laugh at this when you have eaten in that coffee-house, we will reach it soon. How can you go apart and where? How long have you been married? Newlyweds?'

She said, 'Make no mistake. We are not married.'

A desperate recklessness seized Raman. 'Don't believe her, we *are* married.' He glared at Daisy.

The cart-driver smiled knowingly. 'Young people always fight after a night like the last night. It is very common. You were not comfortable. I knew that all along. After a night like that there is always bad temper.'

Raman began to enjoy this situation immensely. Daisy repeated weakly, 'We are not husband and wife. He only works for me. I pay him his wages for working for me.'

Raman said, appealing to the conscience of the world, 'See what is coming over wives these days! I work for her in order to be of help, and now she says –'

She snarled, 'He is a liar.'

'Yes, I am a liar,' said Raman cheerfully.

The cart-driver said, 'See there, he has already forgiven you. This mood will pass. Both of you must be hungry. I will get to the coffee-shop, and after a cup of coffee you will both laugh and embrace.' And he gloated over that prospect.

'This fellow is foul-tongued, doesn't seem to realize what he is saying,' she cried.

The cart-driver suddenly made a deep obeisance. 'Please get back, I will prostrate myself at your feet. We have still time to catch the bus, but if you delay you will be stranded again. I promise to twist the tail of that animal until he gallops for his life and takes you there in time for a cup of coffee, a rest, and then the bus. Please, please.' The man suddenly prostrated himself on the ground at her feet. 'Pray get in. I won't rise until you get in.'

'You should be ashamed of yourself. Such an elderly man to be driven to this. You should not put him to such a trial,' said Raman. With that he gripped Daisy by the shoulder, propelled her to the cart, and commanded, 'Get in, get in now. Come on. You are creating a scene for no reason whatever. You are only hysterical.' He lifted her bodily, pushed her into the cart, and followed her in triumphantly. The cartman resumed his place, started to move; he looked back, gratified, and noticed Daisy sobbing, her face covered with her hands. Raman felt dejected but was trying to look masterful.

The cartman whispered to him, 'Let her have a good cry. It'll do her good. Don't interfere with her.'

Raman, in spite of the erstwhile bravado, was disquietened by Daisy's breakdown of spirits. He wondered if his grip on her shoulder had hurt her. While it gratified his masculine vanity to think that he was really strong, at least stronger than Daisy, he wondered at the same time if he had crushed her collar-bone inadvertently? – that could turn out to be a pretty serious matter. He might have to take her to Dr Anand and put her in plaster. He would tell Anand: Something has happened to my wife's collarbone. Please –. He could picture the astonishment on Anand's face. What! What do I hear? When? When? Dr Anand was one of his oldest friends, and was likely to shout, Bastard! you have gone and done it without a clue to us.

That's all right, we shall talk about it later. First give relief to my wife. He would trill that word 'wife' with pride, let it dwell on his tongue like a drop of nectar. And with the plaster cast on her collar-bone, Daisy would have to depend on him, perhaps leaving aside the population-exploders. She might regret it but he wouldn't. One sure way to win a bride seemed to be to crack her collar-bone gently. He sat opposite, but dared not concentrate his attention on her; he had a fear that if he saw her sobbing, he might himself break down clumsily. It was harrowing to see those firm shoulders heaving up and down, punctuated with a gentle sob now and then. He plucked up enough courage to stretch his hand and pat her comfortingly. But the moment such a contact was established, she pushed off his hand unceremoniously.

She glared at him for a second, hissing, 'Taking advantage! You will learn your lesson like others who have learnt their lessons. I'll see that you go to jail for this. I'll tell the police the first thing.'

While it pleased him to notice her positive spirit reviving, at the same time he was filled with dread. What was she promising him now? He hoped she did not mean literally that she would go to the police with a criminal complaint – that'd be a nice rounding off of his career indeed! The whole town would laugh at him and he'd be unfit to be seen again on his cycle on Market Road; Jayaraj would make capital out of it and corner all the sign-boards. 'You know what that chap did, he tried to molest a customer, when she was stranded on the way, and this chap took advantage.' There was so much evil packed in that single word 'advantage' uttered now by Daisy.

He said, 'Please forget everything. I am sorry, perhaps I tried to joke and carried it too far.'

She just pursed her lips – her small, narrow lip line seemed to have become tighter and shorter. Did she also grind her teeth? If not, what was the noise he heard? Just his imagination, perhaps.

The cartman derived the greatest enjoyment out of this situation. He kept turning round and winking at Raman as if to say, This is all a part of the game. Keep your side up, as ever. It made Raman furious – it was this old fool who had goaded him on to behave in this wild manner – this fellow and the hermit in the cave who gave him encouragement. God alone knew what was going to happen to him when they reached the end of the journey. He hoped there would be no police station in the vicinity of the bus-stand at Koppal. What a mess he had got into! He had a wild impulse to abandon the present company and run away. That'd make a police search for him a definite thing. He decided not to make it worse with further word or deed. Silence was golden. As the bullock-cart bore them along, he lapsed into a grave silence and tried to pretend to himself that he was journeying all alone. The hermit had said, 'You will have trouble before and after.' Did he mean the trouble he was now having? But that might mean that he was going to have later trouble. Even so, it held a promise that, in between the two troubles, he was going to achieve something. Was that it? He pulled his thoughts back – once again moving along the danger line.

Koppal was a little village which stirred itself into activity when a bus arrived at the yard in front of the thousand-year-old temple, now abandoned for public use. A fruit-stall and a couple of petty kiosks stocked with odds and ends came to life at the bus-stop; hawkers, loungers, and mendicants converged on this spot, and melted out of sight when the last bus departed. The cartman was paid off. When he approached Daisy to take leave of her, she spurned him and looked away – as a cause of all her troubles. He stood around innocently, rather bewildered, and drove away his cart in search of passengers who might go his way. Raman tried to carry her bag, but she held it away from him, without a word. She put her bed roll down and sat on it, unmindful of the little crowd standing around. Raman went across the road into the coffee-house and sent a serving boy to ask the lady for her order, and ate his breakfast heartily, alone. When the bus arrived, Daisy got in without a look in his direction and took her seat. Raman got in and occupied a seat several rows behind her. When the conductor came up, he asked, 'Has that woman bought her ticket?'

'Yes.'

'One or two?'

'One,' said the conductor. Raman bought a ticket for himself, thanking God that up to that moment she had not gone near the police.

At Malgudi, she got down first with her bag, hailed a jutka, and went off without a word or look in his direction. Eventually, worrying a great deal, Raman was back home in Ellaman Street.

Part Three

Dreary days followed. Raman was depressed, panicky, and bewildered. He went on speculating again and again whether Daisy would go to the police with a complaint. He was, of course, familiar with the superintendent of police, a friendly man who gave him a nod when they met at the market fountain, where he sometimes came to watch a procession or a political demonstration. Couldn't call him his friend, but knew him. Would that man entertain any complaint from Daisy? On the other hand it was possible there would be a knock on the door, and he'd be marched down Ellaman Street in handcuffs, the neighbours and the customers at the Chettiar shop standing around, gaping and nudging each other and commenting, 'A sign-board painter, after all, should have known his place.'

'What a woman to pick up a fellow like that and encourage him and now goes and complains to the police? She can't be all that innocent.'

'After all, look at her job! Most provocative! She has no better business than enticing innocent fools like this Raman. Poor fellow. His elders such a respectable family. The old lady at home will kill herself now, I'm sure, for shame. All her life she has lived such a religious life. Never missed a single evening's discourse at the temple. Such a person to face this disgrace!'

Raman's imagination had become overactive and he lost all peace of mind. He had not decided how to collect his charges from Daisy now. He didn't want to risk going to her office: if she didn't fling a chair at him, she might call the police. He rued the day that ever brought him to her notice. He'd have to write off this piece of work altogether, and concentrate on his usual jobs. He must start out on his normal rounds again. But he had lost confidence in himself. Felt self-conscious in public. When people looked at him, he felt awkward. He avoided going out, and spent more and more of his hours in his room, moping over some old volume.

His aunt kept up her routine life from five in the morning till ten o'clock at night, when she laid her head on a wooden plank for a pillow, and slept on the bare floor, finding the coolness of the cement surface agreeable. Raman wished he had her stability of mind. She lived like clock-work, performing her duties at home without a question or doubt of any sort. She had been the same as long as he could remember. But lately, he realized, she was worrying about him secretly – ever since he had gone off with the family planner. People known to her whispered about him at the Chettiar shop and here and there, and she did not like the sly manner of their talk; although at first she had liked the girl and admitted her to the kitchen, she was suspicious of her type. Pursuing a young fellow like Raman! No one could say where it might lead, and now after all these weeks of wandering with her, he was home – but looked lustreless. What had this siren done to him? She couldn't guess at all. Although she went about her days as usual without any outward sign of feeling, she was racked with fears and doubts. On that evening when he came back from his tour, he had walked straight to his room, unpacked and changed in silence, eaten his food in silence, never telling her where he had been or what he had seen, as he normally would even when he had returned from a trip to New Extension. He would always describe the people he had seen, joke about something, listen to her own talk, and so forth. But now he was strangely dumb and brooding. She only prayed that he had not got into any hopeless entanglement. Lord Krishna should protect him from that siren. She had ventured to ask, 'Where had you been, all along?'

'Lot of places,' he had replied.

'Was it enjoyable?'

'Didn't go for enjoyment, actually. It was work.'

'Are you tired?' she had asked.

'Could be,' he had replied.

She felt that he didn't want to pursue the subject. She went off at a tangent, which was always easier for her than proceeding in a single line of conversation. 'The commissioner's wife came to the temple. You know those people who used to –' She went on hopping from subject to subject freely, touching upon the past whenever possible – her usual irrelevances in talk. It relieved Raman that she was coming back to her normal state of communication without bothering about him.

On the days following, she noticed him lounging in his room reading, as if he had an examination to face, never going near his work-shed or on his usual rounds of visits. While passing, she stood at his threshold to say, 'That bangle shopman came in search of you.'

Raman was surprised. That 'Strictly-Cash' rejector, and the squeezer of girls' wrists! He had ignored him all these days.

Then she said, 'It seems you promised the doctor's board. He had sent someone in to ask if it was ready. Plenty of people came in search of you when you were away . . .' and she trailed off and went back to her duties.

He was glad to be left alone. He put away the book he had been glancing through and decided to organize his papers, dumped in an old suitcase. Rummaging through them he came upon the little scroll given by the Town Hall Professor. *This will pass*. He kept looking at it, and then carefully folded and kept it in his purse, without any notion why. His torment came from mixed-up causes, panic on one hand, and through a terrible feeling of loss on the other. It was a horrifying prospect that Daisy might never see him again. He felt helpless about it and experienced a loneliness that he had never known before. Life without Daisy's company seemed impossible. He had retained enough sense to ask himself how he could have come to rely so much on this person – the herbal fragrance, the sound of her voice, the movement, gesture, glint in her eye, even the solid silence that she could maintain and impose on her surroundings – these were rich items of memory, and he missed them. He would give anything to revive a bit of that experience. He would love to undertake an endless journey again in a bullock-cart – that had been a rare privilege he could never hope for a second time in his life. What a fool not to have known the value of it at the time and to have behaved like a drunken buffoon! He felt desperate and wanted to race down Market Road screaming, I have done no wrong. Most natural event between a man and a woman. Yet this lady spurns me. She causes me great anguish and has punctured the sails of my life.

Under the stress of this emotion, he quickly composed a verse: 'My sails filled and the boat went forth – but she took out a knife and gashed it; and the boat floundered.' He reread it and wondered if it could be his own composition or an unconscious plagiarism out of one of his rare editions. He went on correcting the lines. A verse worthy of someone accustomed to the sea, but here in landlocked Malgudi it sounded false, and that made him suspicious that it might be someone else's. Anyway, polishing it afforded him a little diversion. He felt he could now understand the outpourings of poets

– the fellows must be in his state of love-sickness or some other agony all the time. His mind went back to *This will pass* – it sounded unreal and irritating. Time would not pass and he would not survive this trial. He lay dormant for a whole week and felt sick of it.

On the eighth day, he shook off his gloom, saying to himself, 'Of course, this will pass . . . it must . . .'; tidied himself up; dressed; and started out on his bicycle. He realized he had been passing through an infantile atavism and fear. When he passed the Chettiar shop, he noticed that the man looked up and stared at him. Raman had an impulse to stop and ask, What have you been hearing about me? Come on, be truthful. He occupied his seat at The Boardless and ordered coffee. He looked around. His friends were not yet come. He was a bit early. The restaurant man cried from his grandstand where he sat and collected cash, 'Not to be seen for days! Where have you been?'

Raman merely bared his teeth in a symbolic smile and said nothing. He knew that most questions of this nature would wilt away if unanswered, the questioner not minding such extinction. Most social talk was such meaningless jabber, which somehow comforted mankind with a sense of communication. He drank his coffee in silence. The standard was as expected. Not deteriorated. After all he had not been gone such a long time to warrant all this nostalgia and sense of history. He had been out only for three weeks, though it seemed ages. His friend Gupta the businessman came in, and shouted in joy from the very entrance, 'Ho! Rare one! Expanding your field of operation, where have you been? What have you been doing with yourself? Tell me the truth, the whole truth, and nothing but the truth.' He took the next chair, beaming at Raman. He looked happy, as if he had retrieved a lost friend. 'Well, tell me what your luck has been?'

'About thirty slogans in different areas, planned now, special rates for eye-hitting large-size letters. No escape for couples wherever they may turn.'

'Have you brought down the birth-rate?'

'Should be down five per cent in a year, which will be creditable.'

'How can you be sure?'

'Well, we can only try and hope, that's all. A medical team will be visiting the areas soon to continue the propaganda in practical ways.' He stopped short, realizing that he was beginning to sound like Daisy.

'Don't you look forward to any addition of your own to the population growth?'

Raman knew what he meant. They had bandied about many masculine jokes on his latest association. But Raman felt sensitive now and repelled by such humour. Gupta noticed the change and said, 'You have lost your brilliance. What is the matter?'

Raman wondered if Gupta knew, and how much, and whether he had any clue about Daisy's possible complaint to the police. He paused as if to give Gupta a chance to say something. When Gupta said nothing, Raman said, 'Lot of tiring travel, that's all. Everything went according to schedule. We found people in the villages responsive and open-minded.'

Gupta, whose hobby was to talk in the tone of an intellectual, was pleased and added, 'Our whole outlook in propaganda must start on the assumption that people are willing to hear you and give a trial, whatever it may be. People are not so dense as city folk usually imagine.'

Raman was anxious that Gupta should not revert to Daisy; the thought of her pained him and made him uneasy. He had thought he might exorcize the obsession if he went out and joked about these matters with his friends at The Boardless, but he realized that he'd rather avoid her name; it seemed too sacred to be bandied about at the coffee-table. He turned the topic. 'We had a difficult encounter at only one place —' and described the temple for barren women and the extraordinary man living in it.

Gupta looked thoughtful on hearing it and seemed suddenly to lose the faith in the people that he himself had proclaimed. 'Superstition, faith, the working of real incalculable forces, all three operate in our country, but we can never be certain where one begins and the other ends . . . we are in a mixed-up state. Social workers have to take this into account.' After his homily he ordered another round of coffee and left.

To Raman this was a refreshing revival, a sense of return to the normal life. After this meeting, he felt reassured. A man-about-town, Gupta would have been the first to hear of it if there had been any police report about him.

Raman cycled up Market Road, took a right turn, and went down Court Road in the hope of meeting the lawyer and getting some money out of him. He found him in the court quadrangle, slowly pacing, talking to a client, with his black gown trailing behind him.

He was probably coaching a witness. Other lawyers were passing up and down in a hurry; litigants from distant villages lounged around clutching bundles of documents. Busy place where nobody had the time to look at Raman or talk to him. But eventually the lawyer noticed Raman and nodded to him, saying to his client, 'Come back on Monday, the stamp-paper will cost ninety rupees.' He said to Raman, 'Long time since I saw you, what have you been doing with yourself all along?'

Raman felt uneasy at the question. Everybody seemed to be asking the same question, as if they had been coached. Could it have any significance? Could his reputation have seeped down to Kabir Street? He wondered secretly, but replied, 'Had to go out of town on business. Have to find fresh business, with prices going up.'

'Yes, yes,' agreed the lawyer. 'Come and see us sometime. I have opened an office in the town over the cotton godown. Come sometime.'

'Don't you want a new board for it?' Raman asked, his professional interest being roused.

'I got one from someone . . .'

Raman felt upset and jealous. 'Who did it for you?'

'Oh, some fellow at the market gate, known to a client,' he replied in an off-hand manner.

Raman didn't like this treachery on the part of the lawyer – that Jayaraj seemed to dog his steps and grab his clients. He said, 'There is a small balance due on the sign I hung up for you.' And held out his hand as if to receive alms.

The lawyer withdrew haughtily: ' This is not the place for you to make your collections.'

'Have I to make a special appointment for it?'

'Yes, of course. I'm busy and you can't expect me to carry a cashbox around.'

Why should you as long as you have your hands in your client's pocket? But aloud Raman said, 'It's a long time and you remember –'

'Of course, of course I remember,' said the lawyer and moved away.

Thank God, you don't remember that I promised to give you a new board. I hope the sand on your name stays on well, you skinflint. Jayaraj is the right man for you.

Next Raman went in search of one of the court-clerks, who was his relative. He enjoyed meeting him occasionally and talking family politics. But today the man was very busy in his office, pointed to a seat on a bench, on which some persons were already sitting, dolefully, waiting for his attention; he was taking documents out of a file and rushing away to a courtroom where a hearing was in progress. When he came back he took his seat and began, 'Sarala's marriage is settled. Curiously . . . it happened this way –' he began, but a buzzer sounded and he disappeared again. Raman watched the faces around him in that gloomy assembly. In greater trouble than I am, he reflected; about to be hanged, perhaps, or lose a property or a home – what a sad gathering! Waiting to know the worst and to get a copy of the court-order . . . That was in the clerk's dispensation, and perhaps he made money out of everyone in trouble – no wonder so affluent now. He was a cousin of Raman's through his aunt, an orthodox bandicoot with a tuft and caste mark. Raman waited, in order to see if the rumours and gossip about himself had reached him – just a morbid desire to chase rumours and verify them. The cousin came back from the chambers and began, 'I heard' – Raman sat up – 'you were out of town.'

'Yes, yes, have to find more business, you know.'

'Yes, yes, of course. I had gone to the temple and met your aunt and she mentioned it. I find it difficult to come as far as that temple, except once in a while, and I was happy to meet her there. She told me about you.'

'What?'

'That you were on a tour.'

'Yes, yes. Have to get more business, you know, with the prices going up and so many bad debts to write off. Fellows get their boards written, but dodge payment.'

'Oh, this is a bad world,' said the cousin, being familiar with the troubles of mankind. The cousin looked innocent, and Raman was satisfied that there had been no back-chat about him nor any police reports. The cousin opened his lips to say something about a marriage again, but the buzzer sounded and he got up and left. Raman also left unceremoniously.

The afternoon was bright and green. Outside the court, he lingered for a while. He had nothing specific to do. Today it was only an exploration. Tomorrow he'd go round canvassing business – he had his well-set orbit for that. So far no mention of the police. So far so good. But perhaps all of them knew he was doomed and were avoiding the topic to save his feelings. This was a possibility. He might be in a fool's paradise with the fetters kept ready for his wrists. Best clear it one way or another. Learn the worst once and for all. He came down the Court Road and passed the town police station. He cycled up and down a couple of times. If there was nothing, he'd be a free man, or if there was the worst to face – well, take it, that's all, nothing could be worse than this suspense. Perhaps they'd let him have a lawyer, and he could get the sandy lawyer to deal with his case . .. thus off-setting the debt.

He passed into the police station through an arch covered with a blue-bell creeper and a short length of walk lined with flower-pots and ferns. Decorated, Raman thought, not bad, as a possible halt on the way to a bigger jail. He ruminated on his present action. Verily like the moth rushing to the candle flame, never waiting for it to come to him, he said to himself. Now one understands why the moth is so impatient to scorch its wings. Assured destruction is better than a half-anticipated one, he thought. What daemon is driving me on in this manner to the police inspector? Even now not too late to turn back, the inspector has not seen me yet, he will as usual be busy writing.

But the daemon propelled him on. He walked up to the little veranda and into the station house itself. A small hall with dark walls and a corner built like a cage with iron bars. Lock-up for miscreants like me, I suppose, he told himself; they'll keep me here for three days.

The inspector looked up at the sound of his footsteps and cried out, 'Aha, the very person I was thinking of!'

Raman's blood turned cold. Sweat broke out. So this is the end, he told himself. He threw a look to his right into the cage-like corner, espied some dim figure clutching the bars, and wondered, My companion, I suppose!

The inspector said, 'Come, come, take your seat.'

Raman obeyed him and said rather awkwardly, 'Good morning. I ... I ... just thought I might see you . . . long time . . .'

'Yes, yes, if not I would have come in search of you.'

Raman's tongue became dry. He essayed to ask, 'You knew my house?'

'Of course, we in the police force can always find the whereabouts of anyone we want. Address of a person is no problem.' Good heavens, how calmly he says that. Now the cat has got the mouse between its paws . . . swiftly reflected Raman.

'If some person is O.V. it can only be a temporary phase, we can always track him down.'

Raman asked rather sorrowfully, 'What is "O.V."?'

'Out of View,' promptly declared the inspector. 'The point is –' he began, but they were disturbed by the sound of the rattling of a tin can near the roof. 'Oh, this damned thing again! Five-Nought-Seven,' he called suddenly.

'Yes, coming, sir,' cried a voice.

Raman said to himself, He is summoning his man.

Five-Nought-Seven, a policeman in semi-uniform, came in and saluted, and Raman rose immediately as if to surrender without delay, but the inspector gestured to him to sit down and said to the policeman, 'That damned monkey is here again,' and the other looked up at a ventilator high in the wall. Raman saw a tiny hand thrust through the ventilator trying to seize hold of a tin can kept there. Five-Nought-Seven glared up and commanded, 'Hey, go away,' in such a stentorian voice that the hand withdrew quickly.

But the inspector was still not able to finish explaining why he had looked for Raman. He began for the tenth time, as it seemed, 'The reason why –' and the rest of his sentence was lost again in the clatter of the tin can. The little hand was once more inside the ventilator. The inspector screamed. 'Five-Nought-Seven! The damned thing is here again. Can't you do something?' Five-Nought-Seven again appeared in his semi-uniform and wildly gesticulated at the ventilator, with appropriate cries. In response the hand withdrew. But the minute Five-Nought-Seven turned to go the rattle came once more with renewed vigour. 'Go and get a long pole and drive it away, I say. Don't be fooling around, Five-Nought-Seven. Get out and do something.'

While he was gone to fetch a pole, a hollow voice from the dark cell announced, 'It's been coming every day. If you light fire-crackers, it'll go – only way. Or if you want to catch it, soak a nut in brandy and put it out for his reach.'

'Hey, shut up and don't concern yourself with all that. We know what to do. Go back.' 'Go back' meant back to the depth of the cell, far into it to the wall. Perhaps the inspector was trying to clear the space for fresh arrivals. Raman was already getting used to the notion of the police station and the world around it. All through this, the rattling went on intermittently, overwhelming all other sounds. Five-Nought-Seven finally came with a bamboo pole and poked it through the ventilator, the hand withdrew, and there was peace again.

The inspector explained to Raman, 'I keep a little Follidol in a tin up there, and the monkey is after it. This is an awful place, infested with monkeys, and if a monkey touches that Follidol, it'll drop dead, and the public will set fire to this station; if it is kept down here, any budmash in custody may reach for it and commit suicide, and the mob will come for us alleging that we have beaten him to death.'

'Why do you want that terrible poison here anyway?'

'To get rid of the bugs which swarm down these walls at night. I have these walls washed with Follidol. If you want to see the fun, stay in that lock-up and you will find a million bugs descending the walls and coming for you after dusk.' Raman shuddered at the prospect. The inspector continued, 'If you look at this crime chart, behind me, you'll see that our lock-up is always full. But I want to maintain a good reputation. I am paying for the Follidol from my own pocket so that these poor fellows in custody may sleep at night; but for Follidol, they would be eaten up. I am also growing a garden. Our superintendent who inspected remarked that this is the best-maintained police garden anywhere. Did you notice the blue-bell arch?'

'Beautiful,' said Raman. 'Why did you want to meet me?'

'I wanted –' but before the inspector could continue his sentence a crowd rushed in holding a man by the scruff of the neck. The inspector sprang to his feet. 'Oh, this blackguard again!' He slapped the man's face and hit him on the head with his cane, ordered the crowd to keep off, and instructed, 'Push him in . . .' Two constables shoved the man into the lock-up, cursing and slapping. The inspector explained to Raman, 'He was let out only today. Already he is up to mischief. Seven convictions.' The crowd jabbered and spoke simultaneously. The inspector picked up his stick and cap, and hurried out saying, 'All right, I'll come and see the spot myself. I must write the first report.' He turned back to Raman and said, 'Don't go away, I'll be back.'

The police station became silent and empty as everyone made for the exit through the blue-bell arch. Raman sat alone for a while, wondering how long he would be expected to stay. If he tried to leave, perhaps they would drag him back and put him in chains.

Five-Nought-Seven came in after his gardening efforts and stood guard at the gate. Raman, as a test, got up and took his bicycle and started out. Five-Nought-Seven would prevent him if he had been ordered so. He just watched and said, 'Going? Well, it'll be late before the officer returns,' and added reflectively, 'Daylight attempt by O.O., and it will take too much time to write the report.'

'What is "O.O."?' asked Raman, unable to contain his curiosity.

'Old Offender, sir,' explained the constable.

A cry from inside: 'I have done nothing . . . you are lying.'

Five-Nought-Seven said calmly, 'He is a desperado.' Raman got on his bicycle and was off.

Fifteen days passed. Raman resettled into his routine life. His visit to the police station had cleansed his mind of all fears. He visited all his clients and picked up his old business. The fear that Jayaraj might have stepped in and snatched away his customers was no longer there. His clients were happy to see him back in business. The soap-nut merchant at the market almost hugged him for being seen at all. The 'cut-piece' cloth-seller hailed him as a saviour appearing just in time; of course, the bookseller loved to see him again for no purpose whatever. Everyone seemed to have missed him, although he did not like the sly manner in which one or two looked at him. That co-operative secretary seemed to be out for gossip as he gave an impression of throwing a significant wink in the course of their conversation. People seemed to know more than they cared to express. However, he could not prevent people from thinking what they pleased. He became a little hardened and felt the better for it.

Raman was also beginning to bother about the fee for his tour which Daisy had promised, and regretted the loss of that big chunk of business that had nearly come to him. If he had done those thirty signs – it'd have made a lot of difference in the turnover. He didn't believe in pursuing money or in sighing over a missed account – but some complex motive and habitual manner of thinking made him feel the loss of it.

Business is one thing, these complications are another, why should one be missed on account of the other?

Even the bangle-seller, that old lecher in the market, had become friendly again. He came in search of Raman and paid an advance for a new sign-board to say NEWEST FASHION NYLON BANGLES AVAIL-

ABLE FOR ALL SIZES. He wanted also a little picture of a veena to be added, for some obscure reason, on the bottom line, and Raman had demanded an extra five rupees for it – in all, seventy-five rupees for five lines – and the bangle-seller had agreed. Raman forgave him all his old lapses, but just asked, 'What about the last bill?'

The bangle-seller, who had behaved so aggressively in the shop, now shrank to modest dimensions and pleaded, 'Between friends there should be no accounts to settle.'

Raman said, 'You could have gone to Jayaraj instead of coming so far. He is just a step away from you at the market gate itself.'

His answer was gratifying: 'In my business, I care for quality and elegance, otherwise I would not be selling bangles, I'd rather hang a blank board than cheap writing.'

That pleased Raman tremendously. The professional side to his nature revelled in rivalry, and success. He was trying to lose himself in all such activities, for if he allowed a little pause, thoughts of Daisy came back, and the pain of separation racked him.

One evening he was at work in the back yard of his home, with the river flowing a few yards away. His aunt was away at the temple. The transactions and traffic of Ellaman Street were coming to an end, as the seller of sweet edible dolls had cried his wares and passed on towards Nallappa's Grove. That meant it was nearer seven than six. Raman had planed the eighteen-by-twelve board smoothly and put on the primary coat of paint, turned it towards the wall to save it from sand particles, and was rehearsing on a small pad the actual lettering to come. Over the short back wall, where sometimes the head of a goatherd would appear, appeared another head now – he became aware of it from a corner of his eye. He turned his back and went on with his work. He ignored it for a long time but getting a feeling as if the nape of his neck had been tingled, he turned round. It took time to understand the import of the vision. Hallucination? Yes, too common when one's mind was obsessed with a single figure. However, the sight thrilled him. He found it difficult to return to the word 'Nylon', which the bangle-seller wished to be emphasized on the sign-board. The danger nowadays was that he was likely to add 'Two Will Do – Limited Family Means . . .' to every message; Ah! Daisy! He looked again to check if the hallucination still persisted. The light in the sky was gone – a few stars were out, and recognition was possible only from the outline. There was no mistake. That large head, the flat forehead, and the pointed chin were unmistakable. She had her elbows on the wall and her face in her hands. He put away his board and pad, got up, approached the wall peering like a short-sighted man. The head was there. He put out his hand to touch it. Solid to the touch. 'Daisy?' he asked.

'Yes,' said the voice in that semi-masculine tone.

He could not find anything to say except, 'Why didn't you call at the front door?'

'I did, no response, so I explored around.'

'My aunt is away at the temple, that's why . . .' He knew he was spinning out a sentence without thought to its sense. He was in a confusion. He began, 'Madam . . .'

'Why "madam" suddenly?' she asked. He had a muddled desire not to offend her in any manner, and he had thought 'madam' would be a prophylactic against it. He said again, 'Why are you here and not at the front door?'

'Have I not told you already?' she said.

'Yes, yes, but I wanted to ask why you have come like this.'

'How else do you expect – with drums and pipes?'

He avoided deliberately, with an effort, the inclination to say, Why not? That's how a bride should come home! He was terrified of idioms associated with matrimony.

I am hardly out of the police station with one foot perhaps still in, he mused. Perhaps she is here to caution me, on second thought, that she has set the police on me and to advise me to run. Perhaps she has regretted her own impulse to betray me.

'What's going on in your mind?' she asked, still gazing across the wall.

'Only that I . . . I missed you . . . you see, I was busy. I've a few urgent works now on hand all of a sudden . . .'

'I was also busy, had to be writing my report of the three weeks' survey.'

'That must have kept your mind preoccupied so that you could not even say good night.'

'When?'

'When we came down from Koppal in that bus.'

'I don't think I said good morning to you that day either.'

'That's true,' he said fatuously.

'Even if I hadn't come tonight, shouldn't you have come to see me to collect your travelling allowance and things like that?'

'Ah, that's all a minor matter. I could always ask you for it.'

'Not unless you signed the form and it was sanctioned at headquarters,' she said, her habit of precise thought asserting itself now.

'Why should we be talking here?' he asked suddenly.

'Because you are found here,' she said.

His mental processes were all tangled up. It still seemed to him incredible that she should be here – unbelievable, it was all perhaps a day-dream. 'Did you come for me?'

'Well, I thought there could be no other reason to come to Ellaman Street.'

'Well, one might come this way to reach the river!'

'Why not?' she said unexpectedly. He hopped over the short wall and reached her side. He was completely self-forgetful – abandoning the 'Nylon' script, forgetting that he had been working since the afternoon and needed a wash and a little combing of the hair. Her invitation cast a spell on him and he joined her. They walked along on the sand, side by side, in silence. They reached the river's edge and went down a flight of granite steps. Luckily no one was there at this hour – though even if there had been, Raman was not in a mood to care. Daisy was here and he was back in her favour – that was all that mattered.

They sat on the last step with their feet in water. It was cold and refreshing. The stars shone, the darkness was welcome, cool breeze, cold water lapping the feet, the voices and sounds of the living town far away muffled and soft; habitual loungers on the river-bank passing across the sands homeward softly like flitting shadows. The air had become charged with rich possibilities. He threw a look at her, and felt drawn to her. He edged a few inches nearer involuntarily.

She did not move away, but said, 'Don't try to get into trouble again.'

He merely said, 'I like you, I feel lost without you.'

'Better than getting lost along with me,' she mumbled on. ' "I love you", "I like you", are words which can hardly be real. You have learnt them from novels and Hollywood films perhaps. When a man says "I love you" and the woman repeats "I love you" – it sounds mechanical and unconvincing. Perhaps credible in Western society, but sounds silly in ours. People really in love would be struck dumb, I imagine.'

'Love is the same in any society,' he said, after all venturing to utter the term 'love.' If she was going to push him into the river for it, well, he'd face it. He said, 'I agree with you. I don't believe in the romanticism created by the literary man. It has conditioned people's thinking and idiom and made people prattle like imbeciles in real life too.' She laughed at this observation, and he felt pleased that he had after all made some mark.

No further speech for a little while. Then his hand seemed to move by itself and find hers, which felt cold and soft. She did not reject this touch, but just laughed and said, 'You are an incurable romantic in spite of what you say!'

'Who wouldn't be, with you so near?' He wanted to say many things to her which would express his innermost feelings, with all the intensity, muddle, and turbulence. He wanted to place his whole life before her in a proper perspective so that she might take him seriously. He rambled on in a reminiscent manner. He did not know where to begin or how to continue. He wished to express to her that meeting her had been a landmark in his existence – how much he owed her; wanted to speak of his philosophy of life; wanted to justify himself as a sign-board painter. A sign-board painter might look ordinary, but he concentrated in his hands the entire business and aspirations of a whole community. He had to explain why he chose this medium, and that took him back further to the starting point, and from there he drifted further back to his college days and to his adventures and romances at that period; how he paid attention successively to a short girl, a tall girl, a fat girl, a lean girl – more imagined than actual. He rambled on incoherently and Daisy listened with patience. He realized that he could not complete any sentence. Ideas got entangled and swung back and forth. In the darkness he could not see her face to judge whether she was listening cynically or with interest. He concluded rather irrelevantly, 'Yes, you are right; I am an incurable romantic.' And added. 'Well, I think I have spoken enough about myself. May I know if you wish to say anything about yourself?' feeling that perhaps she had come there to talk about herself rather than to listen to his biography.

'What sort of information do you expect? Anyway I don't think I can match the grandeur and the variety of your life.' She laughed and continued, 'However, you have known me for months now, and I realize how you must be bursting with curiosity. Now where shall I begin?' She remained thoughtful for a while. 'You remember that cranky old fellow in the temple in that village, who wanted to give a reading of my past? If you remember, he said something that seemed to me rather strange. You remember his saying that he saw me in a hut beside the sea and waves falling on the shore? I don't know how he was able to guess it, but that's where my father tracked me finally after searching everywhere. Don't you want to ask how I got there or why? Neither that hut nor the sea-side was my birthplace. I must go to the beginning.'

Raman sat up, and took away his hand in order to concentrate on what she was going to say. She had never sounded so serious at any time and Raman blurted out, 'Why are you telling me about yourself now?'

'Well, just to pay off the debt of having listened to your own life.'

Raman said, 'I don't think I sounded very clear.'

She said, 'I don't think I am going to sound any clearer; anyway listen to me and don't interrupt me. Much better you know me as I am, rather than have foolish notions. Your narrative has not been of any consequence to me because I didn't have any notion or any curiosity about you, I took you as you came; you did some work for me satisfactorily, as I wanted it, but you behaved – well, well, let us not go into it now. Anyway, let me have my say, and don't interrupt me.' And she narrated the story of her early life in her village home somewhere beyond the mountain ranges and the rivers; she would not be specific about the geography, and he was afraid to interrupt her to seek an explanation. She was not very clear in the sequence of her narrative but he let her continue as she liked, without a question. She spoke of her childhood in some village home where her father owned fields, gardens, and orchards; theirs was a large joint family consisting of numerous brothers, sisters, uncles, sisters-in-law, grand-aunts, and cousins. Of this population fifteen were children. The household was like a hostel; at six o'clock in the morning the house was astir with the children getting ready for the day. Although it was a large, commodious house, children were all over the place. 'I sometimes wished I could be alone; there was no time or place to consider what one should do or think. Practically no privacy. Wherever I turned I would be spoken to or somebody would involve me in a game or expect me to do something or other. The noise at home, which no one else seemed to notice, was enough to madden me: at all times the cry of babies; the shouting of children; the quarrels between some grown-up boys; and the voice of some elder over-shouting all the rest. It was a madhouse. Somehow everything there repelled me. I do not know for what reason since my parents were very kind; my uncles joked with me and petted me; and my sisters, brothers. and cousins were extremely friendly. But I did not like so much common living.'

At this point Raman ventured to ask, 'Could this be the reason why you want our country also to be less crowded?'

She sounded vexed at this: 'I became interested in the population question later in life, but it had nothing to do with my early impressions. Don't connect things in this fashion; I do not believe in such psychological theories. It would not have made any difference to my future, even if I had been the only child at home.' After this explanation she continued, 'All of us were brought up together. We all would get up at six o'clock and immediately crowd around the well at the back yard with tooth powder in our hands, scrambling for the water pot; and we splashed about and washed and jeered and laughed and made a mess and stayed on until my parents or an uncle or aunt came and asked us to get out of that place. Then we were all fed, groomed, dressed, and sent off to different schools in various directions. No single school could take in all of us. Some of us walked across fields, some of us found some neighbour's bullock-cart going that way and took a ride. In some manner or other all of us reached our classes in time. I had to walk a mile and wait on the highway for a bus to the town, where they had a convent school.

'I found my studies dull and lifeless. I was always obsessed with the thought that I ought to be doing something better, something more useful than this routine life; that I was in a vast meaningless organization from which there seemed to be no escape. I had to live like all the other children at home.'

Raman said at this point, 'I never thought you could express yourself so well . . .'

She brushed aside the compliment and said, 'I have told you not to interrupt me. At five o'clock in the evening the process was reversed and all the children converged on the house, ready to devour whatever was available in the kitchen. Once again we were all lined up and fed and washed and groomed and once again we scattered around the neighbourhood to play until it was time to be marshalled back home, to go through our evening prayers; facing the puja room, which was too small to accommodate the whole crowd, we recited holy verses in such a loud chorus that our elders could have no doubt that our voices reached the heavens! And we lined up for a night meal and then good night, sleeping on mats or carpets in various corners of the house with or without pillows, anywhere, and everywhere. All individuality was lost in this mass existence.

'I never dreamt there could be any other kind of life, any other interest in life, any other way of living. I had no idea that it could be changed until the air became charged with rumours of a marriage proposal for me. The other children giggled and taunted me. My father and his immediate younger brother discussed with serious faces what was to be done; there was mention of many letters passing. Studies of horoscopes and talks of details of a wedding celebration. People now looked at me with a meaning; I did not like it. My mother called me one day into a side room and told me to be prepared to be inspected by a prospective bridegroom. They had a shock at home when I told my people that I'd not allow anyone to inspect me as a bride and that I'd rather do the inspection of the groom! They felt outraged and my father's younger brother, my father being too angry to speak to me, took me aside and said, "Don't be mad! Don't you know that it's not done?" I replied, "If it is not done, it's better that someone starts doing it now."

' "What's the matter with you, my dear, why do you want to spoil your chance of settling down in life?" I had to explain that that was not my aim in life. I had other aims. I said that I would like to work, rather than be a wife.'

A statement which sent a chill through Raman. 'I hope you have achieved it, and now you can afford to change your views.'

She ignored this remark and continued, 'I was finally persuaded. I was particularly fond of that uncle and could not brush him aside. I decided to go through the ceremony of being viewed and assessed. I had made up my mind that I'd hate the young fellow and discourage him publicly. They decked me in all the jewellery pieces borrowed from my sister-in-law in the house, diamonds and gold all over my ears, neck, nose, and wrist, and clad me in a heavy sari crackling with gold lace. I felt suffocated with all that stuff over me. I felt sick and felt that I was losing my identity. But I bore it all patiently, as they fitted me out in the side room, and stood around and exclaimed at how well I looked, and the children gaped and cheered and joked. I hated the whole scene. I was seized with a feeling that I was in a wrong world, and that I was a stranger in their midst. I saw my mother's face beaming with satisfaction and I was irritated at her simplicity. Although I was only thirteen, I had my own notions of what was good for me and what I should do in life. Although they admired me, I dreaded to look into the mirror myself. And then they seated me like a doll, and I had to wait for the arrival of the eminent personage with his parents. What a fuss they made when they arrived. It's hard to get a bridegroom, and when one is available parents treat him as a hard-won prize. The young man was not bad-looking, but it didn't concern me. He was a young landlord owning hundreds of acres and earning a lot of money. Seated on the best carpet, the boy's father kept saying, "I have left everything in my son's charge. He looks after everything." He was very fond of his son and spoke incessantly of his greatness, his mother nodding approval to whatever he said. That I was the central figure in all this drama didn't prevent me from feeling amused. I viewed it as a sort of entertainment, and behaved, I suppose, irresponsibly. When the moment came for me to pace before the visitors coyly and reverently – I just strode up like a soldier, the jewellery jingling and the horrible lace sari rustling.'

Raman began to laugh and said, 'Oh, I can see the picture – that mug seated there squirming in his silk shirt and nodding his tufted head with his mouth agape.'

'No, I didn't say he wore a tuft. He had a cropped head, unlike most of the villagers,' she said.

Raman felt terribly jealous of him and said, 'I am sure he must have been squint-eyed.'

'Oh, no, I told you that he wasn't bad as bridegrooms go . . .'

'I am sure he must have been a delinquent of some sort,' Raman said, and added, 'I never knew that you viewed people so critically, or even cared to say much –'

'There was no occasion for me to say anything, that was all, and I don't fish for compliments.' Raman had nothing further to say and remained silent. 'I warned you not to interrupt me, but you are constantly saying things that disturb me.'

'I only wanted to clear up some doubts. Go ahead . . .'

'As I said, I strode up like a soldier marching and stood before the fellow, and he perhaps thought I would knock him down, and retreated slightly. They all looked a little shaken at the very style of my walk. His father seemed so taken aback that he ceased to speak of his son's achievements. My mother said, "Make your obeisance, prostrate yourself on the ground." I shook my head. I have always hated the notion of one human being prostrating at the feet of another.'

'So do I,' said Raman. 'It is odious. I have never fallen at anyone's feet in my life.'

'Don't interrupt me. You can tell me about yourself later,' said Daisy. 'Then the man asked, "What class are you studying in?" A routine question that all would-be brides have to answer modestly. But I turned it round to ask, "What class are you studying in?" And that completely bowled them over, since the bright young fellow did not seem to have got beyond the kindergarten, his only merit and qualification being wealth. They got over this shock, and asked, "Can you sing?"

' "Can you?" I asked. Surprisingly enough, he answered, "Yes, I can." His father explained, "He has learnt from professionals, and his ambition is to perform in Madras Music Academy. Can you sing?" Before I could answer, my father butted in to say, "A teacher comes three days in the week from the town." "But," I said, "I am no good. I am not interested in music."

'It could not go on like this. Plainly the whole proposal had collapsed. Before I could do further damage, they hustled me back to an inner room and a hundred eyes scowled at me. I thought they'd all strangle me. But they left me alone. For days no one spoke to me. I had brought disgrace on the family by my unseemly behaviour. A highly respected family in these parts had been offended and insulted and it was going to be difficult to find a bridegroom for me any more or for the other girls in the family as well. I had damaged the family reputation.'

Daisy stopped suddenly to count aloud as the gong of the Taluk office sounded. She leapt up and was gone before Raman could realize what was happening. He only heard her words receding in darkness, 'Nine o'clock! Never thought it was so late.' He felt angry at the manner in which she had left him.

'I don't know what to make of her, she is a puzzle,' he reflected as he crossed the sands and hopped back to his shed. His aunt was watching him from the back door, and asked in surprise, 'Why are you jumping over the wall? The door is open.' Evidently this busybody had been at the back yard and had unbolted the door. He became cross if his aunt trespassed near his work-shed, it was a tacit understanding between the two that she should not unnecessarily wander around his shed. But she came along occasionally to gather the wood-shavings for lighting the oven. At such times she always sought his permission; otherwise she kept away and the workshop door was to be opened or closed only at his discretion; he was the sole authority in that area. She could open it only when she went across to the river for her bath. Now she had no reason whatever to come up so far unless she was trying to spy on his movements. If she had come up to the back door and opened it, she must have peeped out and seen him on the steps – an uneasy thought. Not that he cared for her opinion. He asked, 'Why did you have to open the door?'

'The street door was left open, and you were not to be seen anywhere and so I got quite anxious.' She went back into the kitchen. Raman realized that it would be no use speculating whether she had seen him holding hands with Daisy. What if she had, what if she hadn't? It was all the same. Holding hands – idiotic pleasure – while Daisy could just wrench herself away and run off without the least feeling. He'd do better than to worry about her. 'What's he to Hecuba or Hecuba to him?' he repeated to himself, some odd titbit floating up from the cesspool of scholastic memory. She should rename herself Hecuba instead of Daisy – one who could behave so undaisy-like. More like emery paper. What if the gong sounded nine? Who would question her? Whom was she accounting to? If there was anyone to demand an explanation, it could only be himself . . . rather a flattering notion. He realized that his thoughts were pell-mell, following her sudden departure, which had frustrated his plan for a tender parting. He had still sufficient self-analysis to conclude, 'To hell with everything. What am I to Hecuba?' and then lit up a lantern and sat down to resume work on the bangle-seller's board He sat hunched up over it far into the night. His aunt knew better than to disturb him at such times. She herself lay down on the kitchen floor and slept. Later on that night, he stood at the threshold of the kitchen, hesitating whether to wake her or not. But she got up and served his dinner. He was afraid for a while lest she might question him; he might have to be both rude and evasive; but when he was nearing the final rice and buttermilk stage of dinner, she just said, 'Krishna's advice to Arjuna on the battlefield was the discourse today, and it thrilled me. The pundit is so learned, you know.'

The bangle-seller seemed to be a changed man. When Raman carried a sign-board for him, he had come to the market dreading lest there should be a repetition of his previous experience, in spite of the affability shown by the man while ordering the board. The shop, as ever, was filled with girls of all ages and shapes. The bangle-seller was clutching a tender wrist but dropped it unceremoniously on seeing Raman. 'Aha, welcome, sir, be seated.' He pointed to a stool in a corner, while all his fawning, chattering customers sat around on a carpet spread on the floor.

Raman unwrapped the sign-board in a routine manner, saying the routine words, 'Don't touch, not completely dry yet,' and leaned it on a wall.

The bangle-seller examined it approvingly. He looked at his audience and asked, 'How do you like it?' And they all murmured, 'Looks nice.'

Enslaved ones, Raman thought, judgement according to His Eminence's views. He said, 'Shall I hang it up for you? I have brought nails – show me where.' The whole company took part in this activity: Raman stood on the ladder to nail up the board, several elegant, bangle-bound hands held the ladder for him, and all the women who had come to buy bangles now stood around watching or placed their hands solicitously on the ladder. 'Be careful, please, we are holding it from slipping, don't worry.' The bangle-seller stood across the path on the other side to study the sign from a point of vantage and uttered many words of appreciation. A small crowd of onlookers also joined. When finally Raman stepped off the last rung of the ladder, he felt like a hero. He almost expected to be offered sweets and to be garlanded with rose and jasmine. He walked back into the shop wiping the sweat off his palm, self-conscious as the spectators stood aside to let him pass into the bangle shop.

The shopman followed him in, saying, 'I'm happy that you have paid special attention to the nylon bangles. Pray be seated . . .' He pointed again to the stool in the corner. Raman's legs ached with the strain of ladder-climbing, and he was grateful for a seat, while his admiring public went back to their carpet. The bangle-seller addressed them generally, 'I'll attend to you in a minute,' turned to Raman, and said, 'Can I get you coffee, Coca-Cola, or Fanta? What'd you like?'

'Thanks, anything,' said Raman and added, 'also I'd like payment of my bill.'

'Now?' asked the bangle-seller.

'Yes, yes, immediately. Seventy-five rupees, less the advance, please.'

'Ah, seventy-five rupees for one board!' cried the man in consternation.

'Yes, yes, seventy-five rupees for one board; one hundred and fifty for two, two hundred twenty-five for three, that's our rate today. I've to change a brush for every fourth line, or hundred applications, and I have given you the loveliest rosewood plank, come straight from the Mempi jungles – even if it's exposed to sun and rain for the next hundred years it won't warp. I have used pure linseed oil and paint from Germany and the sign will stay fresh when your grandson succeeds to your business.'

'Oh, I have not thought of marriage.'

Why not, you have enough opportunities, I'm sure, Raman thought, looking at the clientele. After the shop hour, you have only to keep your hold on one of those slender wrists and it's done . . . but aloud he said, 'I wanted to give you first-class work, and that means first-class material.' Raman enjoyed being back in the professional stream with all that business banter, trade and sales jargon. He felt now that he was regaining his personality, which had been drowned in Daisy-ism, too much of it. Daisy-ism was all right – interesting, titillating, and diverting up to a point – but not to be taken too seriously or tragically. For months now he had been wasting himself in Daisy-ism. I must cure myself of it by constantly questioning, What's Daisy to me or me to Daisy? and lose myself in robust, manly, professional encounters, rounding up the day at The Boardless in healthy company. What if she had come in search of him and sat on the river-step close to him? He was now a hardened man who ought not to attach too much value to such situations. After all, if only he cared to, he could command the attention of all the women of the town, and he wished Daisy had been there to witness how many hands came up to hold the ladder. He knew his personality was not unattractive. He should leave Daisy alone, and shake off this silly burden on the mind. 'You are becoming a contemplative, like a yogi,' said the bangle-seller.

'Yes, yes, my next business demands my immediate attention.'

'What's the next?' asked the bangle-seller, his curiosity aroused.

'Must you know?' asked Raman mischievously.

'Oh, I am always interested in the prosperity of my friends.'

Raman took a diary out of his bag. Its calico was faded, and the year on it was 1962. The bangle-seller remarked, 'It's more than ten years old . . .'

'Why not?' asked Raman. 'I can still use it for ten more years. After all one can write only four lines a day, and not every day, and the diary has three-hundred and sixty pages or more; it'd be a national waste not to use a diary for ten years.' He opened a page and held it up to him to read.

The bangle-seller read aloud, ' "Finance and Investment Corporation", "India Textiles", "Dr Gurunath", "Mathilda Nursery School", "Danger: 440 volts",' and cried, 'Quite a busy writer! Must be making a lot of money.'

'Why not? I never go after business. It comes to me. And the delivery is strictly by turn, that's all. No one can hustle me. You see the date against each item. Even if he is a maharaja, he'll get his delivery only on the due date, and I can guarantee the best material, not like others who pass off soft-wood plank and lamp-black letters!' Raman laughed ironically. He couldn't really explain why he was launching on such a personal account except to impress the gathering in the shop. He was swelling with importance.

This impressed the bangle-seller, and he crossed over to his desk, opened a cashbox and fetched fifty-five rupees, and held them out to Raman with, 'How I wish you could show us some concession.'

'Of course, I have billed you with the discount. Otherwise it would be eighty-five or ninety rupees for fifteen square feet.' There was no sign of the drink offered and Raman said, 'Don't worry, if you can't send for a drink, I can have it on the way.'

'Oh, no, impossible,' said the man and looked at a very young girl waiting to be fitted with bangles: 'Be a good girl. Get a Fanta, tell him I want it.'

While they waited for the girl's return there was a pause, and Raman said, 'Attend to them. Why keep them waiting?'

'Oh, they will not mind,' and his clients nodded in agreement and murmured something pleasant. This chap has cast a spell on them, thought Raman.

The Fanta came, Raman drank it, and got up. The bangle-seller rose courteously and followed him out. Before parting, he said, 'I want a favour from you. There is a lady here, in the birth-control department. Do you know her?'

Raman asked, 'Why?'

'I hear that she is known to you.

'How? Why? How can I have anything to do with a birth-control woman?'

'No, no don't mistake me; one of my customers has seen you in her office, that's all. If you know her, I want your recommendation, that's all.'

'You said you were a bachelor, what's your problem? She is not an abortionist.'

'No, no, not that, not that way, sir. It seems she is going to distribute bangles to villagers as a reward for getting operated on for birth-control. If it's so, please let me do the supplies. I'm prepared to visit the villages and fit them up nicely. Some of my nylon bangles are unique models. If you can come back into the shop for a minute and see for yourself.'

'Oh, no, I can take your word for it.'

'They are unbreakable, and women will do anything to get those bangles.'

Part Four

Now Raman had a fine excuse to knock on the door of Number Seven, Third Cross, that night. Daisy let him in.

He said, 'I won't keep you long, only a quarter of an hour.' She looked rather drawn and tired. Overworked, actually, with no relief, poor girl, he thought. If you had stood by the door and eavesdropped as did an urchin who had brought her her dinner from a near-by restaurant, you would have heard his voice: 'I just came to inquire, on behalf of a friend, if you are offering nylon bangles to village women who –'

'Rubbish!' said her voice. 'We don't believe in that kind of conversion. They must understand what they are doing, and not be enticed in this childish manner. Tell your friend to keep his bangles. I know him. He came here twice with a few samples, and I asked him to pack up and go. I gave him only two minutes. This sort of thing maddens me, I tell you.' A pause and some movement of feet. Her voice: 'No, no, you will be in trouble again. Be sensible.'

'I used to be the most sensible person known at one time. Full of good sense, logic, reason. I could talk the most irrational fellow back into sense.'

'Not to my knowledge,' said the female voice. 'Why not give me also the pleasure of watching your logic and reason at work? I see you only as a rash, head-strong . . . H'sh, don't be childish, let go, you are hurting me; behave like an adult.'

'But you let me touch you on the river-step the other evening!'

'Oh, that! That was different, it was dark there.'

'I can switch off the light here too.'

And then one heard a scuffle and a struggle to reach the switch, feet and hands reaching for the switch, and a click of the switch, off. The eavesdropper applying his eye to the keyhole at this point would see nothing. A stillness followed before the light went up again, the female voice saying, 'If you must stay, please bring your bicycle in. I don't want it to be stolen, or worse, seen on my veranda at this hour.'

'You command, I'm ever your slave.'

'Don't you feel ashamed to say it?'

'No, proud and happy.' And as the door bolt is heard drawn, the eavesdropper vanishes, leaving Daisy's food at the threshold.

All day long Raman went on his rounds of business or sat and painted in his shed. At six he washed and groomed and wore fine clothes and was off on his bicycle. Raman's aunt was bewildered and worried. She noticed the style of dress, and his going and coming. The man in the Sakti Laundry, the one beside the Chettiar shop, now and then remarked to her, 'Your nephew takes great care of his clothes nowadays. Good for us. He wants his shirt pressed every day. There must not be a single wrinkle on it, anywhere . . .' She was hearing rumours. She hardly spoke to anyone at the temple assembly for fear they might talk about him. She discouraged her neighbours or the Chettiar of the shop to hold her in conversation. She connected various titbits of her own observations about him and spoke to him one day while he was finishing his lunch; she waited till the very end before asking, for fear he might stop eating and go away.

'Where do you go away in the evenings?' she asked, unable to phrase her question more diplomatically. Raman remained silent, got up from his seat, washed his hands at the back yard, and hesitated for a moment at the central hall to decide whether to go back to the kitchen and speak to her or go into his room and enjoy a siesta. He felt rather drowsy nowadays during the day-time, but – at five every evening until after midnight revived and bloomed and felt absolutely fresh and active during the hours spent in Daisy's company. Daisy, for her part, nowadays found it difficult to remain awake in her office during the day. Her visitors sometimes surprised her while she dozed in her chair. One evening she said to Raman determinedly, 'You must go back home for dinner, not later than nine,' and unknowingly they chatted and dallied till the Taluk office clock boomed eleven and she got up briskly and showed him the door, and he went out on his cycle swearing, 'That Taluk office gong must be smashed.' But this system did not always work. They ignored the gong on some days, and Raman awoke from their bed only in time to cycle back home before the townsmen should be out, especially before the opening time of the Chettiar shop, which had become of late a sort of watch-tower noting the arrivals and departures in their street. Until this moment Aunt had resigned herself to the situation. Her question annoyed him. He was an adult past thirty and no aunt or even a goddess could ever have the right to question his movements. Why should he feel uneasy about it? Let all the citizens of Ellaman Street gape and wonder, he would not give them any quarter. He would go his own way. Millions of men and women all over the world were going about their normal business without seeking approval or permission of an aunt or Chettiar or any of the hostile and peering crowd of Ellaman Street. This was a wretched part of the town. He wondered for a moment whether he should not sell this old house and take up his residence in a more civilized locality like the New Extension or leave Malgudi itself – this conservative town unused to modern life. But his self-esteem asserted itself and he said to himself, Why should I change my locality or the town – where I have lived since my childhood? Let others get out if they don't like to see me go up and down on my own business, living my own life. The more he thought of his home, the more he began to love it – there was no other spot in the whole town – such a coveted spot by the river, with the breeze blowing. Why should I leave this place?

He hardened himself with all kinds of arguments and re-entered the kitchen. His aunt had her back to him, arranging some vessels on a rack. He stood at the door and let out a slight cough in order to draw her attention. She turned round from the vessels. 'Why are you coughing? Take care of yourself. Don't drink cold water . . .'

'That's all right. I am perfectly well. Well, if you don't know it already, I am marrying a girl – you saw her the other day here.'

Aunt dropped the vessel, as if she had lost her hold on things. She came up to him, '*That* girl! What is her caste? Who is she?'

'Who is she? It is immaterial. She is going to be my wife, that's all that need be known.'

'Isn't she a Christian or something – a name which is . . .'

'Nothing more than the name of a flower, that's all. Daisy is a flower.' He realized that he was not sure what flower it was. 'It's a most lovely flower grown in America, England, and so forth. What is wrong with that name?'

'A Christian! How can you bring in a Christian . . .'

Raman didn't have the patience to launch on the oneness of all religions, but merely said, 'I only know that her name is Daisy. I have not thought of asking whether she is a Christian or what. Never occurred to me to ask, that's all. I'll ask you not to bother about it. She is a human being just like you or me, that's all. I like her very much. I am sure you will also love her. Please be nice to us,' his voice suddenly, unexpectedly imploring and cajoling, for which he hated himself.

But his aunt was unmoved by his appeal. She said nothing, turned round sunk deep in thought, and resumed the arrangement of the vessels. Raman waited for her to begin a discussion of the issue, and was surprised at the turn of events. He never bargained for such a conclusion to his announcement. He felt insignificant and insulted. He wanted her to agree with him or argue with him or start a big fight; but this was too unexpected. He watched the back of her head, then turned round and went back to his den to unroll the mat and sleep. He picked up a book from his collection, a small-print two-column edition of some obscure world history, opened to a page, and ran his eyes down its lines. He did not make out a word of it, but it kept his mind passive and from fretting and speculating about his aunt. He had always counted on the understanding of his aunt and had no doubt whatever that he could always bring her round to his point of view. She had never sulked or even tried to sound like an alien. This was his first experience. His eyes faithfully travelled down the lines of the two columns and then the usual drowsiness overcame him and he fell asleep without any effort.

He woke up at four o'clock, dashed cold water on his face, and went into the kitchen. His aunt was not there; she had kept a tumbler of coffee for him in the hot ashes of the mud oven. He gulped it down, and looked about. She was not to be seen – too early for her to go to the temple. No use worrying about her. Let her be where she pleases. I have done nothing to hurt. I am only trying to shape my life, and I can't really help it if she is going to worry about irrelevant details such as Daisy's religion and such things. She could as well bother about the little dark mole he often noticed on Daisy's right elbow. She had probably gone to the corner shop or to talk to her friends. She had an old friend living three doors off, her constant companion whenever she started out for the temple.

But Aunt always mentioned when she was going out, even if it was only for a few minutes, warning him to mind the door. Now this meant probably that she did not wish to speak to him. Was it the end of a lifetime of association? But why did she make coffee for him if she did not like him? That was a sign of hope indeed, but it might also be nothing more than custom. Anyway he had much to do professionally – he must not lose sight of the fact that he was going to be a married man with increasing responsibilities. With a wife with her own income one had a greater responsibility to prove that one was not going to depend on her. He would have to work harder than ever to deliver signs punctually to his customers, and not give occasion for any comment that he was neglectful or running after women; he had to protect Daisy from such comments. He said to himself, I'll be damned if I'm going to worry about other people's moods or words. After drinking his coffee, he briskly went to his work-shed. He turned round a plank leant against the wall and measured the area to be covered. The message was to be GIRIJA VOCATIONAL INSTITUTE, a women's co-operative institution to be inaugurated by the governor next month. The board was to be completed and dried and delivered within fifteen days. The chairman of the institution was known to him and trusted him, and he would lose his friendship if he delayed the work. Luckily for him the man trusted his taste and did not specify any style of work as others had done. They also wanted him to leave a one-line space for a brief quotation in Sanskrit extolling the virtues of industry, something to serve as the motto of their organization. He didn't care what they had to say, as long as they left the style of lettering to him and did not crowd in too much in the available space. In such matters they should learn good behaviour from Daisy, who had trusted his judgement right from the first day he met her. It was pleasant to think of Daisy again, such a salutary change from the problems confronting him with his aunt. Why couldn't Aunt be like Daisy – so easy to deal with! He was suffering from a momentary forgetfulness of all the travail he had faced before Daisy finally admitted his love. His hands were busy with the letters on the board, a tryout with a soft pencil.

Raman worked on till six-thirty on the plank. Tomorrow he would put on the primary coat, and then the second coat several days later, as drying took time. He didn't trust the quick-drying stuff, which seemed to him just a novelty, unsuited to his work. All done, the board should be ready in ten days. At six-thirty he laid away his task and shut his shop for the day. Urgency had crept into his hours now. He glanced at his watch. He was going to be late today. But Daisy would understand. He'd have to rush to the laundry and fetch his silk shirt and one or two items. As he was hurrying down to the laundry, he saw his aunt arrive – very unusual. He cried, 'Oh, Auntie, not gone to the temple?'

'No. Are you going out?' she asked, implying that she was aware of his routine programme.

'Yes, yes, I'm going to the laundry, must get my clothes before he closes,' and he was off. When he returned a quarter of an hour later bearing his silk shirt wrapped in an old newspaper, he found his aunt sitting in a corner of the hall patiently waiting. He put away his shirt in his room and came back to the hall. She said, 'Ramu, come here and sit down, can't you, for a few minutes? I have to say something to you.' With his heart palpitating, he sat down obediently on the floor, in front of her. He felt as if he had thrown off two or more decades of his existence and was back in childhood, when she used to summon him in order to teach him the alphabet. He could not really decline her summons now. He muttered under his breath: I am already late, but had not the courage to say it aloud as she might immediately retort, 'I know where you are going, doesn't matter if she waits.' Aunt opened with the gambit, 'Help me to go to Benares.'

'When?'

'Within a week, a party will be leaving for Benares, and I'll go with them.'

'Who are the party?' he asked, already a feeling of loss coming over him.

'Andal of the third house is one of the party. She mentioned it some days ago. I just now went up to her to ask if I could go with her.'

'What did she say?' asked Raman, trying to sound casual and lighthearted.

'Yes, she will take me.'

'What a practical traveller you have become, rather like your ancestors who walked up and down to Poona.'

'Yes,' she said rather brusquely, for the first time not elaborating this theme; of late, she had not repeated the Poona trek, which indicated that she was not in a happy state of mind.

'How long will they be away?'

'Three months – they are going to Badrinath and Hardwar first . . .'

'Badrinath! Hardwar! In the Himalayas!'

'They have made all the arrangements – it'll cost seven hundred and fifty rupees!' From this very sordid calculation, she continued, lost in visions of her pilgrimage. 'A dharshanam of the God in Badrinath, and if possible to Amarnath, where the lingam is shaped in ice. I wouldn't care what happened to me or to the world after I have seen the holy places and dipped into the Ganges from its birthplace all along its course, until I end my pilgrimage in Benares. After this I shall want nothing more in life.'

Raman brooded over the financial implications of this proposal. Seven hundred and fifty. His own bank balance was just enough for his venture into marriage, and until the outstanding bills were collected, he could manage somehow. Nothing was due from Daisy until after he had completed the village rounds, which he was postponing until after the rains in September, perhaps until they were settled as a married couple.

Aunt said, 'I have kept in the post office four hundred and fifty, and if you can make up the rest –'

Raman assured, 'Of course you will have it, don't worry. Does it cover your return journey too?'

'Perhaps it does. I have not asked them about it. If I don't do the return journey, I think they may take less.'

'When are they all coming back?'

'This is Masi, by next Adi they should all be back.'

'When do you intend to return?'

'Well,' she drawled, 'that question is not so important.'

'What do you mean, Aunt?'

'It is like this, my boy. At my age, with a few years left, people do not generally want to return. A visit to Kasi is the end. I may live for ten days or ten years or twenty, it is immaterial how long one lives after this stage. It is the ambition of everyone of my generation to conclude this existence at Kasi, to be finally dissolved in the Ganges. That is the most auspicious end to one's life.'

Raman felt dejected and responsible for the banishment of his aunt. He pleaded desperately, 'Don't go, Auntie, stay.'

'This is a chance I have waited for all my life. If I miss their company . . .'

'Nothing is lost, I will make all the arrangements, don't worry,' he said recklessly. She wiped the tears that screened her vision. Raman was too moved to say anything. He had never known a day or an hour without her since he could remember. He appealed to her, while one part of his mind was worrying how Daisy must be waiting and wondering how he was going to explain to her why he was late. He said with desperation, 'I won't marry now, if that is what is driving you away.'

'This is a good opportunity to go with these people, known to us,' she said. 'Andal's company will be there, and we will be happy, I have no doubt.'

'If you want to stay, I will . . .' He was not sure what he was going to say – whether that he would cancel his marriage or postpone it. His thoughts were in disarray. He sobbed like a child and blurted, 'No, I can't let you go away like this.'

She was touched and quietly cried a little herself, and finally said, 'You must live your life, that is all, although if I had known that you were ready to marry, I had a dozen horoscopes offered.'

'You don't understand it, Auntie,' he cried petulantly. 'I am not marrying now because I want to find someone to marry. I love this girl and she will make me happy. Stay, bless our marriage, and then I will make all the arrangements for you to go to Kasi, and you may come back when you like. Even if I marry immediately I will leave her where she is and won't bring her home. You may continue to be here.'

'While you go and live in her house, I suppose?' she asked with some bitterness. She was right. Unless he cut himself in twain there was no possibility of his leaving a part of himself in both spots. He knew it would be hard to be away from Daisy once he was married; even now he felt the hours spent away from her wasted hours. He remained silent. Aunt said, 'I have been hearing all sorts of stories about that girl. Did she run away from her parents?'

Raman overcame his irritation and replied, 'It is nobody's business. She is a rare type of girl, devoted to the service of people, and that is all her religion. I don't know if she cares for any other god or religion, and I haven't asked. Her worship takes the form of service to the poor and the ignorant and helping them live a decent life. She cares not for wealth or luxury or titles. She can live with the poorest in their huts, eat their food, and sleep on the mud floor.'

Yes, that is what I say. Why should you be involved in all this, when officers, judges, and rich men are ready to accept you and treat you like a prince, and give you all the comfort that you may want?'

Raman sighed at the limitations of his aunt's understanding. There was no use explaining to her concepts which were beyond her understanding. He simply said, 'She is a good girl.'

'What is her caste? What is her history? She ran away from home! Don't you know all that?'

'What is wrong in running away? Are not you trying to go away from us now?'

'So you see no difference between me and her? Some maya is screening your understanding.'

Raman overcame the irritation he was beginning to feel. 'Look here, Auntie, you are running away to fulfil your ambition of retiring from the world. She had to run away from an orthodox home where she was expected to . . . no, let us not go into all that. I will tell you what she did, and you will understand. She has told me of all her life. She had to leave home because otherwise there was no way for her.' The sweetmeat vendor's cry and bell approached and receded among a lot of other evening sounds, and the birds were clamouring in the trees. It was very very late, past seven. He must have it out with his auntie today and resolve all the differences, even if it meant going late to Daisy. He wanted to convey all that he had gathered from Daisy about her life, all that he had heard from her in fragments from time to time. He said, 'Auntie, listen to me patiently. Don't interrupt me,' he said, catching the mannerism of Daisy herself. 'This girl's name was Laxmi, Parvathi, Gayatri, or what you will. I never cared to ask. She left when they made her life impossible.'

'Who?'

'Her family.'

'She had her father and mother?'

'Of course.'

'A girl who finds her parents intolerable! Those who are orphaned pray for parents, while this girl –'

'Oh, don't interrupt me,' he commanded again.

His aunt regained her aplomb now. She briskly got up, lit the god's lamp in the little room, and switched on the light, leaving Raman. Evidently she did not relish the story of Daisy. He wished to explain Daisy's biography at great length – how she left home with only the clothes she wore, hitchhiked, travelled without tickets, and reached Madras, her personal safety and womanhood endangered, imperilled, and how she survived and so forth; how she finally studied with the help of a missionary organization, refused baptism but changed her name to some non-denominational label, adopting the name Daisy, how she was trained to live with fishermen in their huts and help and educate them, and then in all sorts of slum areas, how she was thrilled at the first sight of the sea, how she passed her college with the help of a missionary, and was trained in social work and so forth; all her struggles and trials, so moving when he heard them at first hand. Somehow he could not convey it now, it sounded banal. He allowed the biography to fizzle out, and got up, realizing that he was wasting his time. He briskly changed into his evening clothes and left, while his aunt stood at the door and asked, 'Are you coming back to dinner?'

'Yes,' he said. 'I have to see someone on business now, I will be back soon.'

She did not believe him. 'I may go to the temple for at least an hour. If you come earlier, call me . . .'

He came back, however, only next afternoon at lunchtime. All night he had discussed his aunt with Daisy, and all that she had said was, 'Why do you want to stop her if that is what she wants to do? She has her faith, call it superstition if we must, but let her go.'

'She won't come back,' he said childishly and wailed like a child, 'she wants to go there and await death.' Raman felt deeply moved at the picture of his aunt's remains floating away anonymously along the floods of the Ganges.

Daisy just said, 'Tut, tut, don't get so disturbed. What is wrong? If I were an orthodox old person, I would welcome such a life and such an end. On the other hand, she may live longer in those surroundings of peace and regularity. So, Ram, don't make a fuss. Let her seek her life's pattern as she likes.' A passing doubt in Raman's mind – was she tendering this advice in order to clear the way for herself? But he immediately suppressed this and told himself, She has given as much thought to the problems of death, perhaps, as she has given to births – rather an inchoate, woolly conclusion, but it helped him.

Next afternoon when he had had his lunch, his aunt renewed her proposition. Raman went to his room to lie down and browse through a book. Aunt followed him into his room, unusually, and sat down on the edge of his mat. He feared that she might complain of having been made to wait the previous night, but she was graceful enough not to mention it. She merely said, 'Have you thought it over?' She looked more composed than she had been yesterday; the prospect of pilgrimage seemed to have given her poise. 'I spoke to those people and they said that if I was not returning with the party they could take seventy-five rupees less.' She looked like a child promised enough chocolates for the money on hand. 'That means you will have to find me only three hundred rupees. Please write a letter to my bank to send the money order to Benares. If I pay them twenty rupees a month, they will take care of my food and give me a corner for sleeping and resting in a common hall, and the corner will be my own. But who will want greater shelter than the temple and the River Ganga?' She sound ecstatic at the visions of staying on in the presence of Viswanatha. 'After I reach Benares I will write you a postcard.'

'How will you write?' Aunt was literate enough to read familiar sacred texts, but was not familiar with writing except putting her signature on the monthly receipt from the savings bank.

She said, 'There are persons who write for the guests there and post the letters; I will write to you, and you must then send me one hundred rupees, which will be kept as a deposit by the *sabha*, and when death comes, as it must sooner or later, they will perform the obsequies, write to you, and render an account.'

I am hearing too much of death somehow, Raman thought, feeling very disturbed again.

Now she spoke with the cold efficiency of Daisy. 'Well, I don't think I want to live forever. I will be quite happy to leave this world any time. I have done my duty. It was mainly seeing that you didn't miss anything in life . . .'

Raman quickly diverted her talk; he did not want her to launch on a description again of how she had survived with him the train accident which claimed the lives of Raman's parents long ago, while they were out on some journey, a flood having washed off the bridge at . . . He had heard this many times, so often that he had no feeling for the reminiscence, he felt cold and indifferent about it, as if it were a summary of a story on a cinema handbill rather than an accident that involved his childhood and life. And so he said rather hurriedly, 'Surely, you will come back whenever you feel like it.'

She did not give a direct answer to this remark, but asked, 'Will you continue to live here?'

'Yes, of course, where else should I go? I love this place, that's why I want you also to live here.'

Aunt froze at the thought and merely asked, 'Will she like this place? This is an old-fashioned house.'

Raman was pleased at her concern and the chance to speak of Daisy: 'She is a very simple girl, cares only for simple things. How I wish you could see her and get to know her . . .' He became plaintive and incoherent.

'When are you marrying?'

'Soon,' he said and added, 'won't you want to see us married?'

'No,' she said. 'Not necessary, my boy,' she added involuntarily. 'And to think that they came with a dowry of five thousand only six months ago . . .' He didn't like to question her further, and did not like to suppress her or start an argument, when she was planning so thoroughly her exit from home, town, and even life. 'What kind of marriage?' she asked; somehow she had a morbid self-tormenting curiosity to pursue the subject.

'A very simple ceremony.' He did not wish to explain to her that they had resolved to do without any formality. He had explained to Daisy the five kinds of marriage he had read about and they had come to the conclusion that the system called Gandharva was the most suitable one for them; that was the type of marriage one read about in classical literature. When two souls met in harmony the marriage was consummated perfectly, and no further rite or ceremony was called for. Daisy said that although she had no faith in any ancient customs, she would accept it, since it seemed to her a sensible thing. The details of how Gandharva marriage was to be practically realized were left for a future decision. 'We will begin to live under the same roof on any day we decide,' Daisy said.

'And you can call yourself Mrs So-And-So?'

'No,' she had said. 'I won't change my name.' Rather a jolt for Raman, but he did not debate it, and accepted her decision silently. He told himself, In all matters, she will probably be the final deciding authority. Daisy had laid down two conditions before accepting his proposal. One, that they should have no children, and two, if by mischance one was born she would give the child away and keep herself free to pursue her social work. Raman was not to object or modify this in any manner. She explained, 'Long ago I broke away from the routine of a woman's life. There are millions of women who go through it happily. I am not one of them. I have planned for myself a different kind of life. I have a well-defined purpose from which I will not swerve. gave my word to the Reverend that ' would not change my ideas If you want to marry me, you must leave me to my own plans even when I am a wife. On any day you question why or how, will leave you. It will be an unhappy thing for me, but I will leave you . . .' There was a mad glint in her eyes when she spoke thus, but in the intoxication of her personality, Raman said, 'Whatever you say, I will never interfere. I won't question you. I will be like the ancient king Santhanu . . .'

'You always find some ancient model,' she said with a slight sneer. 'Anyway, who was this Santhanu?' Raman narrated the story from the Mahabharata.

Raman got busy making arrangements for his aunt's pilgrimage. He had to meet her friend in the third house to get the precise details. She was a middle-aged wife of an accountant in a local bank who could never come to the point, and she wandered off even more than his aunt while answering questions. The accountant himself was a thin, wafer-like person who sallied out to the bank at ten o'clock and returned at six or seven – staying at his desk, over his ledgers, long after others had left. The lady was the positive part of the household. When Raman arrived, the accountant was starting for his office (a replica of the Common Man created by the cartoonist Laxman, which appeared every morning in a newspaper) with a check coat, an umbrella under his arm, and a slippery pair of spectacles. 'Oh, Raman, how goes the world with you?'

'Thank you. I have come to know about the pilgrimage to Badrinath. My aunt is planning to join your group. You are going?'

'Oh, no, ask my wife about it, I don't know anything about it. How can I go? I have only four days of casual leave left, and the other day our manager said –' Raman switched off his mind. This was an office-ridden negative man who could think and talk of nothing but office matters. No wonder the lady wanted to run away to the Himalayas.

On hearing voices in the street the lady appeared at the threshold and unceremoniously cried, 'Ah, Rama, come, come,' ignoring her husband completely, and the man slipped away without a word. The lady was hefty, with a bun of half-greying hair tied up high over her nape, large cheeks, heavy jowl, and a turmeric-splashed face. At the sight of her Raman felt reassured. Thank God, she is the type who will push her way through and lead my aunt up the Himalayas and take care of her. She spoke so loudly that their conversation could be heard in the opposite row of houses. Raman made his inquiries, and the lady said, 'I will take care of her, don't worry. She is vexed with you even if she is not showing it outside.'

'I don't want her to leave now.'

'Why not?' asked the lady aggressively. 'Why do you prevent her from realizing her ambition of a lifetime? Till now she had the responsibility of cooking and looking after the house. Now you are going to engage another cook, and so why should she stay?'

Raman regretted that he had made this visit. The talk was taking an unpleasant turn. He wanted to announce that Daisy was not going to cook for him. She was a special kind, worth a hundred of the mugs around who called themselves wives and mothers. He wondered how it was going to be possible for Daisy to live in the midst of this company. Speculated why he should not move to Daisy's flat, a neutral area. But he dismissed the idea. He was deeply rooted in these surroundings, and he was obliged to no one in being there. Let others keep out of the way if they didn't like Daisy – who, however, could be counted upon to manage and survive all conditions of existence.

Through a great deal of loud and irrelevant talk he got all the data regarding the pilgrimage, but it was a trying experience; often he was on the point of turning and sneaking away, like the husband. It was the extreme garrulity of this person that must be sending the accountant bouncing off to the bank so early each day, and he wondered how his aunt was going to stand this companion for months to come, until they parted at Benares. They were leaving on Wednesday next, five of them, and two sons of another family were to be their escort; a payment of six hundred and seventy-five rupees immediately would settle everything. The money could be paid into the hands of this garrulous lady and she would attend to the rest herself. Raman promised to see her again, went to his bank, and collected sufficient cash from his own account to pay for his aunt's entire trip. He did not wish to have her use any of her own money, although she had said she wanted only a small sum to supplement her own savings.

He came back to the garrulous lady an hour later and gave her the cash. Again she met him at the threshold and launched on the state of the nation and other such topics and all the good things his aunt had done for him – how they would both be missing the evening discourses at the temple, and how unwise Raman was not to have married when a good dowry was coming, and what was this rumour she was hearing about his marrying someone out of caste, who was she? He said there was no truth in such rumours – a white lie was the easiest way out of this garrulous encounter, giving no room for further arguments. This lady was known to him since his schooldays and to him the most acceptable part of her was her devotion to Aunt. She had much influence on Aunt and for decades, as he could remember, helped her with her shopping, outings, advice, and philosophy, and was her inevitable companion at the temple every evening. Raman suspected that she was also the channel for all the gossip about him that reached his aunt. He wanted to use her influence now and requested the lady, 'I hope you will be bringing back my aunt when you return.'

'How can she come back to your house? After all, her desire is to spend her last days in Kasi. Let her; don't interfere with her plans. She will be happier doing what she likes to do. You think you can do what you like and command her to stay and look on. No, my boy, you are mistaken if you think that we will be slaves of the family all our lifetime. No, no, there is a limit to forbearance. One can't –'

He diverted her talk by giving her the cash to count, explaining, 'I am happy to be giving her *my* money,' putting emphasis on *my*.

'Why not?' the lady cried, 'after all that she has done for you?'

He added weakly, 'She wanted only three hundred rupees from me, but I am giving her the full amount, not touching her cash.'

'You are a good boy,' she said and added, 'You will go to heaven for this, I am sure. You are a gem, don't I know, but evil company warps – that is why it is important that one should marry at the proper time and age. Nothing can then go wrong. That is what I told your aunt. I told her, "You have brought this misery on your own head, you fool. Why did you let him roam about like a well-fed colt? Naturally –" '

Raman said, 'Is there anything else that I should do?'

'No, no, young colt, this is all. I will take care of the rest, we will buy the rail tickets and do everything. Considering my family affairs, I wish I could also stay away at Benares.'

'Probably Mama is hoping you will,' he remarked and ran down the steps, without affording her the privilege of the last word.

Aunt's preparations to leave were elaborate. Although her possessions could be packed into a small jute handbag, her instructions were never-ending. Raman became very considerate and spent as much time as he could with her. He felt he owed her at least his company. He curtailed his visits to The Boardless and visited Daisy in the evening for only a couple of hours, unless she asked him to see her earlier at the office. She was still his best customer, and got him to do various small sign-boards for hanging out in select spots. Aunt was really pleased to find him at home in the evenings. The weight on her mind seemed to be lessening, and the unnatural silence that she had exhibited a few days ago was gone. She had become loquacious and reminiscent as before, repeating the story of her grandfather's Poona days several times. She visited the temple in the evenings as usual – she did not wish to miss certain important episodes in Krishna's life. And by the time she came back Raman would also be back from his visit to Daisy; while serving dinner, Aunt spoke to him of the story she had heard in the evening. 'Do you know when Krishna revealed himself to the maidens, every one of them, thousands of them, felt convinced that Krishna was there dancing with them. How it was achieved the pundit explained, also its inner significance . . .' From this she would switch to instructions about household matters. 'Remember the rice in the bag is cleaned, and all the pebbles and unwanted things have been picked out . . .' All afternoon the rice was one of her major occupations. She would put on her glasses and, with a heap of rice from the basket spread out little by little, by the light of the afternoon sun pick up chaff and stone and all unwanted things, sitting on the back veranda. 'You won't have to buy gingelly oil for at least six months; the Chettiar just got freshly harvested sesamum crushed at the oil mill and gave me the best stock, but you must see that the lid of the jar is taken off for a few minutes at least once a week, and then it won't become rancid. You must be careful to watch it while the lid is open. You must be careful to see that insects don't get into it, and you must tell whoever is going to look after these things.' This was her manner of referring to Daisy, always indirectly and wanting to forget her if possible. 'And then take care to air the pickles and preserves at least once in ten days; and remember there is enough stock of dried vegetables to last you for two years; don't waste any of them.' Raman was getting an inkling of the enormous industry at home that had gone on unseen in minute detail, to keep him properly nourished day after day for thirty years. Aunt had no other occupation but gathering fodder for him night and day and keeping them in proper condition. He was aghast at the amount of work involved.

She packed into her jute bag her possessions: a couple of white saris, a little brass casket containing sacred ash for smearing on her forehead, a coral rosary for prayers, a book of sacred verse, and two tiny silver images of Krishna and Ganesha. 'These were given to me by my father,' she explained.

The jute bag had room for more, and Raman suggested, 'Still a lot of space – why don't you buy a few things that you may need on the way?'

'I don't need anything; there is just space enough for my shawl, and a small bundle of parched rice, enough to last for two weeks.' She mentioned, 'They say that we can get parched rice anywhere in this country, and also buttermilk and bananas. What more could I want?' She had lived on one meal a day for years, as he knew. He marvelled at the simplicity of her life and her minimal wants. He had had no occasion to observe her so closely, and her way of life was a revelation to him. He brooded over her life and mission: She seems to have existed only for my sake. Except the evening visit to the temple, her world was purely and totally dedicated to his well-being. She had stayed at home, waiting to feed him, watching his moods to know if he was happy and contented. When he went out she waited to open the door for him; when he spent all the evening with Daisy without coming home, she must have been in an agony.

She said, 'The milkman comes with the cow at four-thirty in the morning. Someone must watch him otherwise he will add water.' Raman now realized that if the curd and milk had been pure and creamy, it was only because she stood up beside the cow at dawn, peering into the milking pail. He had taken so much for granted all these years! He was like a plant, tended with care, unaware of the continuous labour involved for the gardener. While he had been happily painting sign-boards or gossiping at The Boardless or gallivanting with Daisy, so much had been done backstage to keep him alive. It'd been a lifetime of dedication for another being, actually. How would Daisy fit into this scheme? Would she stand beside a cow at dawn, or keep the oil jar aired regularly? Unthinkable. She had made it very plain that she couldn't be expected to do any of those things. He wondered how Aunt could keep away from all this activity and from her own world of grains and what not, in which she had been involved for a lifetime. He pleaded in a sudden access of tenderness, 'Come back from Benares; stay there as long as you like, but come back, to your own home. This is where you should be. What'll you do in Benares?'

'I've told you what I will do. Nothing else matters. I have drifted in the ocean of samsara for countless years, don't you think?' She seemed to be carried away by the simile, doubtless picked up during the evening discourses, and drifted on with it. Then she returned to mundane matters: 'Don't give up the Chettiar shop. He's a good man; and ask him whatever is required, and he will get it, even if it be milk from a tigress's teat. The vegetable-seller comes mostly on Tuesdays; we owe her –' She went out to the veranda and counted the horizontal lines marked with the juice of a green leaf on the white wall, and came back to declare: '– We owe her three rupees and fifteen paisa. Don't pay her more; that will settle her account up to date. Beyond that it'll be up to you. She generally appears around ten o'clock in the morning. Will you be there? Will *anyone* be at home?' She meant Daisy, perhaps, implying that she was not the kind to stay at home awaiting vegetable-sellers. Raman was irritated by Aunt's insinuation but in the mood of farewell forgave her. The old lady went on, 'You see, on Fridays, I usually drop a ten-paisa coin into the money-chest kept at the temple. Never failed even once these thirty years since I came to this house to look after you. That god protects us, remember. You may put the coin in whenever you pass that way; otherwise, you may tell our neighbour to do it for you.'

Raman's aunt had left three days ago. For Raman, the house seemed to have become vast and full of echoes. He diverted himself by peering into every part of it and planning alterations for Daisy's coming. This home on the river was to be managed by Daisy hereafter – no, she disliked the term housekeeping; she wasn't going to do that. During their evening discussions, she had quite often remarked, 'You will be as much a housekeeper as I'll be. What does that term mean anyway? It makes no sense to me. I don't like all this obsession with a house and the keeping of it.' Home was a secondary matter, the primary one was work.

Preventing conception is the only subject of importance, I suppose! Raman reflected, but did not utter it. A home, in Daisy's view, was only a retreat from sun and rain, and for sleeping, washing, and depositing one's trunk. Her possessions were limited to this ideal – in some ways, very much like Aunt. If Aunt's worldly possessions could go into a little jute bag, Daisy's filled a small tin trunk and a BOAC air-travel bag which the missionary had given her before leaving for the Congo. Her furniture consisted of a folding chair, a stool, and a small bamboo table full of nails. She had a roll of mat and one pillow, and slept on the hard floor. Raman had once suggested to add a grace to living, 'Why not have a few simple items of furniture?'

She shook her head. 'Not for me. These have been my furniture for years and are quite adequate. You may do what you like for yourself . . . I don't know.' He did not mind her own bare minimum in all things. But what disturbed him was her habit of separating 'his' from 'hers' and her lack of interest in any joint venture. She didn't even try to convert him to her point of view. It shook all his notions of a life of 'togetherness' but he told himself, That is her constitution, mental make-up, like the curve of her nose or the straight line of her lip, and can't be helped, and not my business really. Such things do not matter in love.

All this should have suited his way of living too. He himself slept on the floor too, but on a mattress; she dispensed even with the mattress. 'Why should we live differently from a million others? I have lived in a hut and know how our people really live,' she would say. But after she came to live with him, he hoped he could cajole her to lie on a mattress, a separate one for her if she was likely to object to a double mattress on the floor. He himself did not mind or notice that he had slept on a mat whenever he spent the night at her apartment. Now why should he think of all sorts of new things when they were to become husband and wife – terms which he could not pronounce before her for fear of upsetting her. She would go on saying, 'Nothing extraordinary for a man and a woman beginning to live under the same roof.' It rather bothered him, but he accepted everything she said. He realized that the path of peace lay in not contradicting her. Two drivers cannot be at the steering wheel of a motorcar, he often thought. He was quite prepared to surrender himself completely to her way of thinking, and do nothing that might leave him in the plight of Santhanu. No questioning and the wife stays, but any slight doubt expressed, she flies away forever. He had agreed even to surrender their hypothetical child, just to keep her in good humour.

Raman went through his house to make sure that it was clean and spruce. He had the kitchen wall scrubbed and whitewashed. A whole week after Aunt's departure was taken up in these tasks. However undemanding Daisy might be, it was still his business to provide her a tidy home. The old mud oven which had served them would no longer do. He got an electric hot plate, discreetly moving the old oven out of sight, to be kept only out of sentimental considerations. Most probably, he told himself, I shall be the one to work in the kitchen, and let me fix it to suit my convenience. He bought aluminium and glass utensils; the ancient rice-pot of bronze could have only an antique value. The little room beside the dining-room, hardly ten feet wide, had served as a puja room for his aunt. This was to be allotted to Daisy; she could put up her table and folding chair, and keep her office papers and files. The room had a small window which admitted enough light and air. If she wished to be isolated, she could shut the door, and he could knock, if he needed her; he would keep his own room with his books and roll of bedding untouched. He could order another roll of bedding stuffed with pure silk cotton for her, his room could accommodate both the beds on the floor, and they could feel cosy like a couple of birds in their nest. He had a passing idea that he should name his home 'Nest' and hang a board on the door; the banality of the name could be mitigated by artwork; he'd choose a design and calligraphy indicating the branches of a tree in whose fork two birds nested. And when the eggs came – no, the surrender would not come at the egg stage, only when it was hatched; she could prevent it at an early stage; but somehow she wanted to wait for the baby to come and then hand it over to a home. If another baby came the next year, again another gift; and if she displayed the normal fecundity of our country-women, she would be handing out babies at a fast rate to a hooded nun or a bearded bishop in some charity home! And no question asked, at the slightest hint of a query, she would melt out of sight and be gone forever. She was indeed a great puzzle at every turn. Sometimes he paused to wonder how he was going to carry on with her a whole lifetime, without any knowledge or understanding of her at all. He was perhaps making a fool of himself by this marriage. But it was Gandharva-style marriage, as easily snapped as made. In any event they'd have to go up before a registrar, if not for anything but to protect the child's nomenclature. The child was not to come, and so why worry, what a muddle? Whatever it was, their signature before a registrar would be inevitable.

Aunt's puja room in the process of conversion into Daisy's room was stripped of the gods she had worshipped and left behind. Now Raman took them off their stand and stored them away in a cupboard.

Daisy paid him a visit rather unexpectedly late one afternoon. He took her round the house explaining the various improvements he would be making to suit their needs. She took no interest in the changes planned and often remarked, 'Everything seems to me all right as it is. Leave them alone.'

But he said, 'Leave me alone to set up this house for our comfort. I won't listen to your advice on this one subject.'

'Please yourself,' she said and lapsed into silence as he kept describing how he was going to colour the walls of the hall, the scheme for the kitchen, and so forth; she nodded mechanically to everything he said. When they peeped into the puja room and he had said, 'This'll be your room, you can put up the table and chair,' she looked in and remarked, 'I remember seeing your aunt's gods on the stand here, where are they?'

'Safe in that cupboard there,' he said.

'Is it safe?' she exclaimed in a mock fright. 'Will the gods not smite us for this effrontery?' Raman laughed at the notion, rather loudly and artificially. Following this they engaged themselves in theological jocularities.

'Can you lock up a god?' she asked.

'Why not?' Raman said, falling into the mood.

'What locksmith can produce a lock strong enough? While human safe-breakers work their way through the strongest lock, can't a god do as much?' She seemed to be in an extraordinarily frivolous mood now.

'Why, would you be afraid to stay alone in the room? I'll transfer them to another cupboard in the hall.'

'You find a story for every occasion in the puranas. Have you none in which the god in the almirah comes out and twists the ears of the man?'

'More likely the god will come out and give the woman a child — such incidents are common in the Mahabharata, of gods straying among mortals and producing demigods,' Raman said. He wanted to sound a note of the utmost blasphemy in the hope of gaining her approval. 'Well, we might create a story on those lines. After all, someone like you and me will have produced all those stories.' He wanted to sound super-rational, although he had not really made up his mind as to whether the legendary gods were real or imagined allegories. In any case when he remembered the absolute faith his aunt had displayed and her acceptance of a Divine Will and the various forms of divinity, he said, 'Anyway, my aunt has complete trust in the gods and possesses greater serenity than anyone else I have known.'

'If so, why move the gods? Leave them undisturbed in their old place,' she said lightheartedly.

They were now at the threshold of the room. The street door was shut and bolted, and the hall had dim light from the ventilator high up, a beam of the afternoon sun coming in from somewhere. Far off over the river leaves of a peepul tree rustled; the atmosphere of poetry and half-lit privacy suddenly provoked his desire. He shot out his arm and tried to seize her. She shook him off unceremoniously with, 'Time and place for everything. What is the matter with you?'

What a fool I am not to have noticed her mood! he said to himself. Smiling mood and non-smiling one, talking mood and silent one, caressing and non-caressing. How on earth am I to judge when to do what, when to say what, and how to do the right thing at all times? Big problem for me, since I do not wish to offend her in any manner. He quickly drew away from her and assumed a prosaic business-like tone. 'Can't help a few changes to suit changing conditions. However, I hope you will feel comfortable in this room.'

'Yes, yes,' she said. 'Of course, no need for you to worry too much about anything. I'll be all right.'

'This is your home as much as mine, and so don't have any hesitation.' She remained silent when he said this; he pointed out the small front hall and said, 'If you like we may order a few chairs, and you may receive your visitors here, if you like.'

She just said, 'Let them come to the office, no visitors after office hours,' with finality. He showed her the kitchen and the hot plate he had fixed. She looked at it all without comment. He was dying to know if she approved of the hot plate. But she said nothing. Making food and eating seemed to her worthless occupations.

'After all,' he said apologetically, 'we must have a place like this kitchen so that —'

She cut his sentence short with, 'I can pick up anything, anywhere, to eat. I am not particular about eating, cooking, or storing things. Millions of our people have nothing to eat all day. Anyway, any sort of food from a restaurant will be adequate for me.'

'Yes, yes, that's true, after all, restaurant-keepers are professionals, full-time food-makers. No need for us to bother about such things.'

'Waste of energy,' she added. He wondered if at any time she would say 'Let *us*' or 'we' instead of 'I' and 'me'. He threw his mind back to recollect, but she specified everything for herself and always seemed to say, 'Do what you like, I don't care and I do not need your attention or arrangement.' What sort of married life is this going to turn out to be? Separate lives and separate everything! Only the roof was to be common, and perhaps the bed – even of that he was not certain how long. She might want to lock herself in her room and forbid him to enter. Should he write a NO ADMISSION sign and present it to her as a wedding gift? These thoughts coursed through his mind, as an undercurrent, while he tried to talk over details. He wanted to ask at this point whether he could get a small dinner table, just sufficient for two, but checked himself. She might reiterate her contempt for food, and the plight of the hungry millions and that might upset *him* and drive him to say something, a rash joke perhaps, that might upset *her*. Dutifully he led her to his room, with its roll of bedding on the mat floor. All that she said was, 'You and your strange books!' He suppressed his desire to declare that he intended to make it their bedroom. Time enough to settle it. He had a fear that she might even say, 'I will stay in my own apartment and you stay here and we will meet by appointment, from time to time moving equidistant from either end.' This would surely be a most original way of living as a married couple.

He then took her to the back yard. She peeped into the well and then across the short wall at the river: 'I love this river behind your house.' He noted with some slight pain that she still said 'your' house, rather than 'our'.

'This is my work-shed,' he said rather unnecessarily, pointing at the planks, wood chips, and the cans of paint.

When they came back into the house, she sat down on the mat in his room, leaning on his roll of bed, and stretched her legs. 'Tired?' he asked solicitously, sitting down at her feet, careful to give no hint of making a pass at her. He noticed her feet were unattractive and the skin had cracked at the heels. 'Do you walk barefoot?' he asked.

'Yes, when necessary,' she said. Her proximity and that peculiar aroma of some herb about her were intoxicating, but he held himself away resolutely. As if reading his mind, she said, 'You don't have to sit so far away, come nearer if you like.'

He grinned gratefully and moved up and sat beside her, leaning on the roll, and gradually his arm encircled her shoulder and he said softly, 'Now I feel better. After all we are a married couple.' He avoided the words 'husband and wife'. Such a precaution seemed to please her, and she nestled close to him and let him caress her body. She shut her eyes and remained still. It was a moment of profound harmony between them. One part of him was afraid to speak for fear it might tear the gossamer-texture of this moment, but the practical part of his mind urged, This is the time to clarify matters, don't waste it. He whispered, 'Are you sleepy?'

'H'mm, h'm,' was all she said without stirring.

'I want to ask you something.'

'What?' she asked almost inaudibly.

He said, 'When do you want to move over here?' No reply. She was breathing softly, rhythmically. He kept looking at her for a while and repeated his question and added, 'Now the house is ready, you know.' Another pause, silent, rhythmic breathing. He waited and asked again, avoiding every trace of impatience, 'Are you giving thought to it?'

She nodded. He again waited, and she murmured, 'The tenth will be all right. The lease for my flat is to be renewed that day . . .'

'Not at all necessary. You may close it. I'll get Gaffur's taxi, good fellow, I know him. It'll hold all your things, and you can move first thing in the morning – six o'clock in the morning?'

'Make it eight,' she murmured.

'So the tenth, at eight o'clock; must tell Gaffur. Today is the seventh . . .' he repeated, becoming incoherent with joy. 'We will not have to be running after each other any more –' He was not quite clear as to what he wished to say, but concluded, 'Obviously we won't be separated, isn't it so?' He waited, but she had fallen asleep. Poor thing, must be feeling exhausted, must have something for her to eat and drink, when she wakes up. He was overcome with tenderness. He stroked her gently, letting his hand rest on her breasts; as he watched, her face wore a serenity he had not noticed before. Her angularities and self-assertiveness were gone. He was struck by the elegance of her form and features, suddenly saw her as an abstraction – perhaps a goddess to be worshipped, not to be disturbed or defiled with coarse fingers. Very gently he withdrew his hand and edged away. But she suddenly turned over on her side and with her eyes still closed, threw her arms around his neck and drew him nearer and lay unmindful as his fingers fumbled with her clothes. He was overwhelmed by her surrender and essayed to whisper, 'This is our true moment of consummation. No need to feel stealthy or guilty any more, under my own roof. The bride has come home.'

*

On the evening of the ninth Raman went to Daisy's office. She was apparently counselling a group of women. He waited in the corridor, and as soon as the women trooped out, went in. Daisy sat in her chair and looked up inquiringly. Raman had believed that a subtle intimacy had been established between them and that she would carry traces of the earlier afternoon's ecstasy about her. But she displayed no such sign, and remained aloof and official, after motioning him to a seat. He felt as if it were their first meeting and he was there to take her order for a sign-board. He explained, 'I was passing this way. I'd to deliver a board to . . . in this same building downstairs.'

'Have you done it?' she asked, once again the precise business-like automaton, functioning within an iron frame of logicality – cold and aloof like an eagle circling high up in the skies.

'Yes, I have also received the money for the work – nowadays I am business-like, have to be, you know!' And he simpered uncertainly.

Daisy didn't smile, but said, 'Those women you saw now, they are from Nagari.' She unrolled a chart and said, 'Mainly mat-weavers and forest-dwellers there . . .' Looking at a report she added, 'The situation is alarming. Its population was just nine hundred last year this time, today it is just around twelve hundred; that means a thirty-per-cent increase.'

'A lot of nuptials must have occurred,' Raman said, unable to contain himself. She looked through him without a smile. 'It is a serious matter, you know. Something must be done immediately about it. Those women are coming back to take me there this evening. I must go and see what's happening.'

Was she going to force her way into every bedroom and shoo the partners apart? But he asked aloud, 'Do you want me to go with you?'

'Not necessary.'

'No wall messages?'

'No. Not suitable for them. Literacy is only one per cent; direct talk is the only possible communication.'

'Do you mean to say that you will speak to everyone of the one thousand two hundred?'

'Why not? I can, if I live in their midst. I am wiring to Delhi to send a medical team immediately. In all, the total population to be covered would be . . .' She hardly looked at him, completely absorbed in the statistics before her, drawing a pencil over a sheet of paper and adding up. 'An average of – mind you it is only an average – four hundred adults in each village may have to be sterilized or fitted with contraceptives, and at least twelve villages in this lot. That is attending to about five thousand in all in this sector. And then I shall move further into the interior, perhaps on foot, as no roads are likely to pass through those forest villages.' She was like a general, planning a campaign.

Raman asked dolefully, 'Do you see an end to it?'

'No. How can there be an end to it? There are a million villages in our country and even if I devote myself to this task every day of my life –'

She was soaring on the wings of statistics which, it seemed to Raman, had had a damaging effect on her mind, and he just said, 'You can't be worrying about everyone in the world. Well, do your bit and let others also help.'

'I am not concerned with "others" or what they do. The missionary has trained me to avoid thinking of others and to carry on as well as I could. I do not know any other method.'

'What about me?' he asked pathetically.

'What about you?' she asked without lifting her head from the calculations.

He said quietly, 'Tomorrow is the tenth, and at eight a.m. I'll bring Gaffur's car to Number Seven, Third Cross, to take you home.'

She remained silent for a moment and then said, 'Well, it doesn't seem to be possible now.'

'Why?' he asked, his heart sinking.

'You see why . . .' she said.

He was shocked at her coldness and cried, 'Have you no feeling? Have you no memory?'

Now she put away her papers and looked up. He felt an impulse to grab her by the shoulder and shake her up, but it seemed impossible in this office. She had an official armour that discouraged any such attempt. If nothing else, the desk came between them. He contented himself by shouting, 'I am, am I not, your husband, asking his wife to come and live with him as agreed? And you pretend as if that question is unimportant! Come on, tell me what am I to do now?'

'You have your work, go on with it. You have your world, in which you have always existed happily, even before you knew me. It is always there, isn't it?'

'When are you coming to live with me, or are you not? Give a straight reply.' No sooner had he said it than he regretted it.

Her reply to any tone of challenge was a foregone conclusion. She merely said, 'This is an office and don't shout here. Those women will be coming in any minute and I don't want you to create a scene before them.'

He flourished his arms wildly and cried, 'Let them come, and I will tell them that we are married by Gandharva rites and night after night we have slept together until yesterday – and today you are the champion of the poor masses. If you ask me to get out of here, I will stand in the street below and shout till I gather a crowd.'

'If you want to do that sort of thing, it will be . . . well, I don't know.'

She looked crestfallen for a moment and then left her seat, came round, and took his hand into hers. Her aura and the herbal fragrance calmed him momentarily and he sobbed, 'May I come with you?'

'No, this is the end.'

'I'll in no way interfere with you, live as you live, in the open or in a hut, walk barefoot in the forest paths, seek nothing, demand nothing, I will not mind any hardship if I can be with you. Please . . .' He felt abject and mean saying it, but desperate to move Daisy's heart.

She repeated, 'No, this is the end.'

'Won't you ever come back to me, my house is ready, it will always be open and ready for you.'

'Let us face the fact,' she whispered, her breath wafting on his face. 'Married life is not for me. I have thought it over. It frightens me. I am not cut out for the life you imagine. I can't live except alone. It won't work.'

'Will you never come back? Some day, will you promise to think it over, my door will be open . . . know that.'

She gave a squeeze to his wrist and said, 'Don't hope for it, it won't work. Today I am going to those villages in the forests and may not be free for three years. I have told you, five thousand men and women have to be taken care of immediately. After that they may move me elsewhere – even to Africa. I cannot afford to have a personal life.'

'Won't you come back to this office?'

'I may not; they will soon be finding another person with whom you may arrange to collect your dues and do further work. This time

I have asked them to send a man for this office and that will save you from complications, I hope . . . please understand me . . . calm yourself . . .' He could hardly believe that he had possessed her only forty-eight hours ago. She said, 'I want to forget my moments of weakening, and you must forget me, that's all.'

'Don't you realize how you have disrupted my life, with my aunt gone . . .'

'This has helped her in a way; after a lifetime of domestic slavery, she has freed herself. Why do you grudge her that in the few years left for her . . .'

'For your sake I have locked up her gods.'

'Well, bring them back to their pedestal, before you begin to feel that they resent you and are punishing you with madness. The gods, if they are there, will look into my mind and judge whether I am choosing the right path or not; if I am wrong let them strike me dead. I am prepared for it.' This was her first serious reference to the gods. He was overawed by her logic, shook off her hand, and turned to go.

'Would you like me to help you with the packing?' he asked.

'All done,' she said, moving away. 'They will be fetching my things now.' She went to her desk and gathered her papers and files, while he stood uncertainly, his wits half paralysed. She went about her work unconcernedly.

He began, 'Daisy . . .'

'Yes?'

He did not know how to proceed; he had no words coming. 'Daisy, you can't leave me like this.'

She looked up and said, 'Calm yourself. You will be happy married to someone very different. Seek a proper partner for yourself . . . you can, any girl will accept you – no, adore you. You are everything a girl dreams of.' For the first time she was sounding so emotional and personal. He noticed, at least fancied, that her eyes were misted and her thin lip twitched.

He feared that he was driving it hard for her, and felt a sudden compassion. He asked, 'If you found me so good, why do you abandon me to someone else? How is it possible? How can that be done? I don't understand it at all. I think I'll go mad if I try to understand you. That day as you lay, on my mat, in my room, in my embrace, did you not agree to make a move and start our home life on the tenth, that is tomorrow?'

'At some moments, and moods, we say and do things – like talking in sleep, but when you awake, you realize your folly . . .' she fumbled on, unable to state it all very clearly. 'Oh, forgive me for misleading you . . .'

First time in her life she was humbling herself. Where was all the regal hauteur gone? He felt pleased that he had dented her armour. He pleaded again, 'Which proved that you could abandon yourself at a moment – when you are overcome with love: you have shown a tremendous storehouse of the love, you can give a fellow new life; why do you want to kill that great gift within you?'

She merely answered, 'Because I have a different life chalked out.'

'By whom? Who has chalked it out?' he cried.

While her hands were gathering her papers, she said without looking at him, 'I can't answer all that now. Do me this great favour – don't again talk of the past or think of it. I am wiping it out from my mind. I can . . .'

'Oh, yes, I know you can. But I'll not let anyone forget it. I'll declare to the whole world what we have meant to each other. I swear, I will. Let those three women come, they will be my first audience.'

'Poor fellow, you are going out of your mind.'

'Yes, you are the cause, you have shattered my intelligence. You are bringing confusion to me. I am in a –'

Further statements of his mental state were cut short by the sound of footsteps on the stairs. The three women entered, one of them saying, 'The car is ready. Your box is in the car, we gave the key to the main house as per your instructions.'

'Three women! Unlucky for anyone – not a chance. Three witches of Macbeth, the sisters of Fate – when they arrive in threes, your fate is sealed,' he declared loudly, glaring at them, and then asked imperiously, 'Anyway, who are these?' with a touch of distaste as if they were intruding into his domestic state.

Daisy, with one hand still picking up papers, pointed with the other to each and mentioned their names. 'They come from different places, but in each centre they are our honorary workers, and they are doing wonderful work in their areas.'

'Still, a thirty-per-cent increase of births at Nagari, how do you account for it?' he asked.

They looked a little abashed at this comment. 'There are many causes for it, sir. We can't go into details at this moment. We'll presently investigate and give a report . . .'

'It won't happen again,' said Daisy.

'Who is this gentleman?' One of the ladies asked, overawed by his authority.

Daisy promptly said, 'Oh, he is a . . . a . . .' She was searching for an appellation, and when Raman opened his mouth to speak, she looked nervous and gestured to him to be silent.

But he quietly announced, 'A painter of signs and, and . . . what more shall I say?'

Daisy intercepted, 'An artist in lettering. He's been a great help to me.'

'You won't believe it if I announce really what I am,' he said.

Daisy bustled about noisily. 'Oh, those windows. Mr Raman, please lock them for me.'

Raman ran up and bolted the window and the door to the balcony and then darted up and snatched the bundle of papers from Daisy's hand. 'Let me carry them for you, madam . . .' She looked puzzled. The three women trooped down the staircase. Daisy stayed back to lock the office door on the landing. The three women were gone out of sight.

Raman could not resist the opportunity in the semi-dark landing. He dropped the paper bundle and clutched Daisy to his heart, saying, 'I'll love no one except you. Understand, you are my wife. Come back to me. I'll keep the home always ready for you.'

'Let me go,' she said. 'Oh, the papers are scattering.'

'I'll pick them up for you, darling, come back to me.'

'Leave way, they are waiting.'

'Promise you will come back to me. I'm your husband, promise . . .'

She was scared of him now, but still said, 'I can't promise anything.'

'*Whenever* you change your mind, come . . .' He stooped to pick up the papers.

She said, 'Ram.' He stood up, his heart aflame. 'Give this key to the watchman of this building.' While passing the key, she gave a warm grip to his hand and took it to her lips, then, dodging him, raced down the stairs. The other three were already seated in the car. Raman held the door open for Daisy and handed her the papers.

'Ready?' asked the driver, turning.

Raman hailed: 'Oh, you old owl Gaffur at the wheel? I hoped to call you tomorrow, but never mind . . . Take the ladies safely. Just a moment, Gaffur, you know what I feel like doing now?'

'Yes, Ram, good to see you. What do you want to do?'

'Drive a nail into your tyre.'

'Always boyish! Why?'

'I don't know. Don't ask for reasons. Good-bye, ladies,' he cried, as Gaffur's ancient Chevrolet roared and belched smoke and jerked forward.

Raman had a last glimpse of Daisy as she sat back, almost withdrawing her face into the shadow. He reflected, Maybe we will live together in our next Janma. At least then she will leave people alone, I hope.

Raman took out his bicycle. Waited till the Chevrolet turned around the fountain and disappeared in smoke in the direction of New Extension and on to the mountain road. He looked at the key in his hand. 'To hell with it,' he said, and slung it into the dry fountain – an act which somehow produced the great satisfaction of having his own way at last. He mounted his cycle and turned towards The Boardless – that solid, real world of sublime souls who minded their own business.

BY THE SAME AUTHOR

'Like Paul Theroux and V. S. Naipaul, Mr Narayan has a faultless ear for the intricate eccentricities of Indian English' – *The Times*

'Narayan's is a voice of great distinction' – *Sunday Times*

Malgudi Days

Here Narayan portrays an astrologer, a snake-charmer, a postman, a vendor of pies and *chappatis* – all kinds of people, simple and not so simple, drawn in full colour and endearing domestic detail. And under his magician's touch the whole imaginary city of Malgudi springs to life, revealing the essence of India and of all human experience. 'A treat ... he is an enchanter' – Hilary Spurling in the *Observer*

Talkative Man

Bizarre happenings at Malgudi are heralded by the arrival of a stranger on the Delhi train who takes up residence in the station waiting-room and, to the dismay of the station master, will not leave ... 'Compulsive and enthralling quality of narrative' – *Sunday Times*. 'His lean, matter-of-fact prose has lost none of its chuckling sparkle mixed with melancholy' – *Spectator*

also published:

A Tiger for Malgudi	**Under the Banyan Tree**
The Vendor of Sweets	**The Guide**
The Man-Eater of Malgudi	

Essays	*Memoirs*
A Writer's Nightmare	**My Days**

and

The Ramayana

A Shortened Modern Prose Version of the Indian Epic